THEIR WANTED BRIDE

A BRIDGEWATER BRIDES NOVEL

RAISA GREYWOOD

BRIDGEWATER
BRIDES

Cover design: Bridger Media

Cover graphic: Hot Damn Stock; DepositPhotos: kyslynskyy

BRIDGEWATER BRIDES

Welcome to Bridgewater, where one cowboy is never enough! *Their Wanted Bride* is published as part of the Bridgewater Brides World, which includes books by numerous authors inspired by Vanessa Vale's *USA Today* bestselling series. This is a steamy standalone read. Enjoy!

ACKNOWLEDGMENTS

I'd like to first thank Vanessa Vale for inviting me to write in her fascinating new world. I hope I've done her stories justice.

A huge shout-out also goes to Engineer Hubby, Mr. Greywood, for his unwavering support and faith in me. Literally, this amazing man drove me to Texas and back, without complaint, all so I could research a Western. He's just that awesome. Love you to the moon and back, baby.

———

Want to see what I'm up to now that I've returned to the present from 1880's Montana? Join my Raunchy Renegades at https://www.facebook.com/groups/272762356598383/.

You can also sign up for my newsletter at https://www.subscribepage.com/bridgewater.

As a bonus, everyone who signs up will receive a FREE exclusive Bridgewater short story based on the events in Their Wanted Bride.

PROLOGUE

ALEB

"I SUPPOSE it's time for me to choose who I'm about to marry." Maddy pulled a shiny silver dollar from her pocket and tossed it, then caught it out of the air. "Call it."

"Heads," my best friend Justin said.

She opened her hand, revealing the tail side of her coin, then set it gently on the table. "That means you'll do the honors, Caleb. I suppose we ought to find the preacher before it gets too late. Thankfully, I won't need a ring."

"Why not?" I asked. "Most ladies want to tell the world they're married."

"They get caught on things. It's a good way to lose a finger. Aside from that, I'm not seeing either of you wearing one."

Infernal woman. My cock ached when I thought about taming that sass. I caught her arm and spun her to face me. "You're going to wear a wedding ring, Maddy. You can take it off for working, but I'm going to tan your backside if I catch you without it when you aren't."

Her pretty eyes widened in surprise, and I had to hold myself back from kissing that sweet mouth.

"Why do you care?"

Thank goodness we'd had the foresight to request a private dining room in the hotel restaurant. Pushing her against the wall, I cupped her cheeks and crushed my lips to hers. She tasted just as sweet as I thought she would. The scent of her lemon soap swirled around me, making me growl as I sucked her lower lip into my mouth. Maybe I ought not be kissing a woman not yet my wife, but it was the only thing I could think to do to quiet her.

She stiffened and tried to wriggle free, but as I nipped her lip and stroked away the sting, she relaxed against me and wrapped her arms around my shoulders. Whimpering softly, she stood on her toes and pushed a hand into my hair, her slim fingers tugging my head lower.

Biting back a disappointed groan, I pulled away, soothing her with one last brush of my mouth over hers as I passed her to Justin. Taller than me by more than a few inches, he remedied the height disparity between him and Maddy by picking her up off her feet, making her straddle his thigh.

His large hands cradled her backside as he kissed her thoroughly enough to make her whimper. I liked hearing that sound, and I especially liked seeing her wrap a slender calf around Justin's hip. Her skirt rode up, revealing a swath of pale skin and a trim ankle encased in a battered leather boot.

Leaning close, I nipped the shell of her ear, then whispered, "Ride him, Maddy. Let Justin make you feel good."

Reaching between them, I opened her bodice, loosening the buttons one at a time until her pretty bosom was revealed to us. Pert and a generous handful, her rosy pink nipples beckoned me to taste. My mouth watered, but I held back so I'd have something to look forward to on our wedding night.

Neither of us would claim her until after we went before a preacher and bound her to us. That didn't mean we couldn't give her pleasure beforehand.

Justin backed up a step, pulling her away from the wall. "Get behind her," he muttered.

I took my position facing Maddy's back and snaked my hands around to cup her breasts. When I traced my thumbs around those sweet pink morsels, she arched and tossed her head, crying out as her nipples furled into tightened buds. Rolling them between my fingers, I kissed the tender skin under her ear as her hips bucked against Justin's thigh.

He grabbed her skirt, pushing it to her waist to reveal her pretty cunny framed by white eyelet drawers. Her russet curls were damp with arousal and I gritted my teeth, wanting nothing more than to claim her. Justin was having every bit as much trouble controlling himself as I was.

Banding my arm around her waist, I held her still and jerked my chin at him, giving tacit permission to touch her. I didn't think I had enough control left to make sure I didn't go too far.

He traced a gentle finger down her belly and kissed her, swallowing her cries. When he reached her pussy, she spasmed against him.

"Please," she whined. "I need—"

"We know, darling," Justin murmured. He reached under her skirts and her eyes flew open as she let out a soft squeal of delight. He must have found the little bundle of nerves at the apex of her sex. Fuck, she was a passionate little thing.

"Come for us, Maddy," I ordered. "Let us see you take your pleasure from us."

Jerking hard, she exploded with a soft scream, her chest and face turning red with exertion. I swiped a finger down her bare thigh. Just as I thought...wet. Copious moisture slicked her soft skin. I was desperate for a taste.

After licking my finger clean of her spend—sweet and tangy just like her—I kissed her damp forehead as I put her bodice to rights. "That's just a sample of the pleasure we can give you."

Justin smoothed her hair, tousled from our loving, then tucked a wayward curl behind one ear. Touching her chin, he brushed a soft kiss over her trembling lips.

Struggling to open eyes glazed with what was probably her first bout of passion, she let out a soft sigh of repletion. "Heavens, it must be a sin for a body to feel so good."

Fuck, it *had* been her first orgasm. She'd get more from us. And soon.

Justin set her on her feet, wrapping an arm around her to help her keep her balance. Turning to the side, he adjusted himself in his trousers, wincing as he cupped his swollen cock. He was probably in the same agony I was currently suffering.

I did some adjusting of my own, then said, "I reckon we better find that preacher, Miss Madelaine. Won't do our reputations any good to be caught kissing a woman who isn't our wife."

Her eyes closed sleepily as she touched her swollen lips. "It's Maddy. My husbands should call me Maddy."

1

J USTIN

Two months earlier...

"ONE MORE STOP, then we'll head back to the ranch," Caleb, my best friend, said, striding purposely toward the mercantile. His blond hair gleamed gold in the late February sunlight. Tall, with a muscular frame, he walked as if he owned the world.

My folks worked his family's farm, and we'd been inseparable since we were barely out of swaddling. There were days when I missed that old homestead in northeastern Ohio, but Caleb had his eye on moving west for as long as I could remember.

Not all Caleb's ideas were good ones. He'd gotten us into more trouble than any two little boys ought to be allowed, but he always took the blame. I guess our respective parents figured I didn't have the imagination for mischief. I had plenty of imagination, but my mama threw a mean switch. Smiling at the memory, I followed him inside.

What with the train making a stop in town, real businesses had cropped up, including a small hotel with a good restaurant, a mercantile, and even a postmistress down the street from the saloon. Bridgewater was a right nice place to be, especially for me, the son of an escaped slave and an abolitionist. The townsfolk didn't give a whit about the color of a man's skin. Their needs were simple and straightforward. They provided for their women and would stop at nothing to care for them.

It was odd at first. I'd always believed marriage was supposed to be between one man and one woman, yet the men of Bridgewater decided that wasn't good enough. To them, two men were needed to satisfy a woman's every need in bed and out. To provide for her and protect her, slake her darkest desires...

Shifting my feet, I attempted to control my thickening shaft at the mere idea of taking a wife for our own. I couldn't fault their reasoning. If a woman's husband died, there would be another to keep her safe and provide a stable home for her and her children.

It was one thing to share a soiled dove. We'd done that many times, and left our partners blissfully sated. I couldn't stop daydreaming about embracing the custom brought to Montana from Mohamir by English soldiers who wanted to find a new home in America. Someday, Caleb and I would find our own bride. We'd use one of the carved wooden toys to prepare her back passage, making her ready for both of us, and she'd blossom like a flower under our touch.

Letting out a breath, I got my head out of the clouds and

focused on what we were doing. "What do we need? Far as I know, we have plenty of beans, flour, and coffee."

"You'll see." A wicked smile crossed his face and he bellied up to the counter.

"Good morning, boys," Mr. Rutherford, the shopkeeper, said. His partner, Mr. Thompson nodded, and returned to arranging shelves. Their wife, Laurann, a pretty lady with dimples and curly blonde hair, smiled at us from her spot behind the till. "What can we do for you?"

"I want to place an ad in the newspapers," Caleb replied. "Justin and I are looking for a wife."

"No, we're not!"

"Trust me. I have an idea." Caleb winked at me, his expression reminding me of all the times he'd gotten us into trouble as boys. I swear, my mama must have worn out her arm giving us our lickings.

"Oh, that's exciting," Laurann said, her brown eyes sparkling. "I'll let the reverend know y'all are fixing to have a wedding."

Sighing, I rolled my eyes and resisted the urge to remind Caleb about what happened the last time he got a wild hair and decided to take a wife. Truth be told, I wasn't too sorry about that. It hadn't occurred to us to share a wife back then, but Carrie objected to our friendship and demanded he choose her over me. She was spoiled and willful, and had her eye only on Caleb's family farm. Thankfully, she'd shown her true feelings before the wedding.

"I thought you were done having ideas," I muttered, knowing I was going to go along with his plan. Nothing would come of it, but if it made him happy, I was willing to let him have his fun.

His face tightened as if he'd heard what I didn't say. "We're gonna do things different this time."

Blinking, I scanned the words he'd written, then laughed outright. "You got dropped on your head as a baby, didn't you?"

His face reddening, he grinned and handed the paper to Laurann. "Aren't you tired of sleeping alone? Don't you want a wife between us to keep warm during those long winter nights?"

Damnation. I nodded as a flush of heat traveled down my spine to lodge in my balls. "Wouldn't that be fine? Not sure asking a woman to bring nothing but a horse and saddle is going to get us a wife though."

"I got a feeling about this," he replied, grabbing a few cigars from the bin on the counter and paying for them.

"Maybe we should go back to that brothel in Butte and find Tessa. Remember her?"

He smiled fondly at the memory, but shook his head. "I sent her a letter. She's already married to a homesteader in Oklahoma."

"I'm happy for her." Tessa was a good girl with iridescent blue eyes and a heart as big as the heavens. She deserved the joy of a husband of her own.

We left the store and retrieved our horses. Caleb's mare snapped, making him dance out of the way of her teeth. "I have a good feeling about this. Should have done it months ago. I'll wager she shows up before the weather turns, and we'll have ourselves a wife. In fact, when we get home, I'm going to get started on building our marriage bed."

Laughing, I caught my own horse against the hitching post and jumped gracelessly into the saddle before he threw me. "Better make it a big one," I advised, "I got a powerful need to give our wife some loving."

The idea of getting a woman, *our* woman, between us made my cock hard. Who would claim her first? Would

Caleb want her pussy while I took her ass? She'd scream her pleasure, calling out both our names as we made her come while she rode our cocks.

What would such a woman look like? She'd be tall with generous curves, and strong enough to bear the two of us as we fucked her to sated bliss. She'd have brown eyes and plump lips sweet as honeycomb bowed up into a perpetual smile Caleb and I would put on her face after a night of hard fucking. We were generous lovers and we'd see her well satisfied. Day and night. Straightening my shoulders, I led the way out of town, spurring my horse into a lope. Maybe it was a fool's dream, but sometimes Caleb's feelings were right. If that meant we'd get a bride, then I was all for it.

———

MADDY

"No, no, no, Madelaine! A lady glides when she walks. She does not tramp about like a hired hand."

I made one last attempt to catch the book perched on my head, then flinched at the sharp whistle of a cane cutting through the air. A line of fire lit up my bottom, making me bite back an ugly curse as the heavy bible hit the floor.

Biting my lip against a pained cry, I kept my silence and knelt to pick it up, then straightened my spine. I refused to give Celeste the satisfaction of watching me rub away the sting from that blasted cane. My light cotton day dress did nothing to soften the harsh blow, and it would probably leave another welt on my backside.

Contrary to her words, the heels of Celeste's smart boots beat a tattoo on the oak floor of the parlor as she marched up to me. "Your father's last wish, God rest his soul, was to see you suitably married, and you take every opportunity to thwart me."

Celeste wasn't worth the trouble of an answer. The men she presented were boring as dry toast. They wanted a pretty girl who would stay silent and bear children. I was sure it was necessary one like her husband, but vague distaste was the best I could muster for my stepmother's choices.

I wanted a husband, but being silent and biddable was not one of my gifts. My future husband didn't have to be handsome or wealthy. I wanted someone who could make me smile like I had a secret. My best friend Dahlia grinned and blushed every time her husband Reggie laid a gentle hand on the back of her neck and stroked a finger across her jaw. I got an achy, hot itch deep in my belly when I watched them together.

What would it be like to share a man's bed? I'd seen horses mate uncountable times, but I thought it must be more. A hurried rut wouldn't make Dahlia smile like that.

Celeste swished the cane at my face, making me jump backward and stumble over a chair. "Have you nothing to say for yourself, Madelaine O'Connor?"

That was enough of that. Celeste had put one too many lines on my bottom, some of which had scarred. Narrowing my eyes, I caught my balance and snatched the cane away from her. Breaking it over my knee, I said, "Yes. I'm not a child anymore. If you hit me again, I will shove that cane so far up your backside you won't have to worry about your posture ever again."

I dropped the pieces at her feet and left the house, ignoring her shrill screeches. The situation was quickly becoming untenable. I'd been stuck inside with her for days with idiotic lessons on being a lady, and I was tired of it.

I'd never liked Celeste, and the feeling was entirely mutual. We'd been able to hold a tenuous peace while Daddy had been alive, but she wanted to remarry. No woman wanted a pretty stepdaughter around when courting a fellow. I understood that, and judging by the leers from some of the men coming to call, I'd be wise to make myself scarce.

The house I'd grown up in would be mine and my husband's when I married, but I didn't care. The place had ceased being a home the minute Daddy brought Celeste to live with us when I was barely ten. I wondered if I should just pick someone and have it done. Being married to a man I didn't actively dislike had to be better than living with Celeste and her string of suitors.

When I reached the stable behind the house, I kicked off the painful slippers Celeste had insisted on and shoved my feet into riding boots, breathing out a relieved sigh when I wiggled my toes in the worn leather.

Smiling, I listened to the quiet whicker of the only thing on Daddy's land I truly cared about. Fishing a lump of sugar from the bowl in the tack room, I went to visit my best friend in the world.

"Hey, Prince." I stroked my stallion's velvety soft muzzle as he searched my hand for the treat. "Celeste is being her usual horrible self. I'm sorry I haven't been to visit."

He nodded his dished face as if he understood, rubbing his head against my shoulder in commiseration as he chewed the sugar. The palomino stallion had been a gift from Daddy for my sixteenth birthday, bought at an auction from a man who didn't know the gem he possessed. I knew a fine blooded Arabian when I saw one, as had Daddy. Prince was lean, leggy, fast as lightning, and smart, but he wasn't a Kentucky bred Thoroughbred.

Prince's true value was only now being recognized here in Kentucky. His foals were highly regarded as excellent saddle horses with uncommon good sense. I leaned against him, sniffing back a tear as I remembered Daddy making me promise to marry the first man Prince liked.

Maybe a ride would clear my head. I led him from his stall and tacked him up, grimacing at the sidesaddle. I hated it, but didn't want to return to the house for breeches.

The crisp early spring breeze caressed my face, and I smiled. It was nearly impossible to hold on to a bad temper on such a gorgeous morning. I held no illusions the situation with my stepmother would improve, but at least she might have enough sense to keep her damned canes away from me. I rode past the general store and nudged Prince around, deciding to stop at the hotel and get something for a picnic lunch.

I kicked my foot free of the stirrup and screeched when someone plucked me from the saddle and set me down. Spinning around, my crop in my hand, I scowled at Nathan Bergman, the owner of Lockerbury's only saloon.

He was handsome enough, and not too old—like some of the others Celeste had presented. Nathan might have made a good husband if he wasn't so... Well, dishonest and a little seedy, truth be told. It wasn't so bad he kept a certain type of lady in his upstairs rooms and cheated at cards, but he watered his bourbon. To a born and bred Kentucky girl, that was a mortal sin.

"Can I help you, Mr. Bergman?" I asked, only just managing to keep the tartness from my words.

Nathan tipped his hat, somehow making the polite

gesture appear lewd. "Well, I expect you can, Miss Maddy. See, your mama—"

"Stepmother," I corrected. "And my name is Madelaine."

His face tightened, but he kept a toothy smile firmly in place. "Be that as it may, your mama and I have mutual interests."

"And what might those be?" I wasn't sure I wanted to know, but asked the question. By the determined look on his face, he was itching to tell me anyway.

"You, pretty lady." He took off his hat and bowed his head. "I'm in fair desperate need of a wife, and your mama has her heart set on seeing you happily married."

"Not interested." I loosened Prince's girth and looped his reins over the hitching post. Nathan Bergman was decidedly not a man who could give me a secret smile. The thought of his touch was repulsive. "I'd think you and she would suit better than you and I would."

Reaching out a hand, Nathan stroked my cheek, brushing a strand of copper hair away from my face. "I'm not interested in Celeste," he murmured. "She doesn't hold a candle to you, sweetheart."

I backed out of reach, carefully putting Prince between us. "Thank you, Mr. Bergman, but as I said, I'm not interested."

Nathan smiled, baring his teeth. "I think I can make you interested," he replied. "There's another part I haven't told you."

Prince rumbled out a low nicker, crowding against me as he shifted his hindquarters toward Nathan. "I can't imagine what would make me change my mind."

"Celeste is one step ahead of you, my lovely fiancé." Nathan's smile never wavered as he stepped around Prince. "She knows how attached you are to this nag, so she sold him to me. You can either be a good girl and come along with him, or I'll sell him off to a glue maker."

I blinked and barked out a laugh. "Why on earth would you consider such a thing? Aside from that, Prince isn't hers to sell. He's mine."

I had no intention of telling Nathan Prince's true worth. He'd likely force me to the altar at gunpoint. Of course, that was what he was attempting, but it wouldn't work.

"Ah, that's where you're wrong, little one. Everyone knows how much you dote on the beast. What better way to convince you to do as you're told?" Lifting his hand, he tugged my hair, pulling hard enough to hurt, then smirked when I jerked out of reach. "Your daddy's will says everything belongs to her until you get married, God rest his soul." Backing away, he raised both hands and added, "Go look for yourself if you don't believe me, but I'll be by in a few days to collect my horse and my new wife."

Staring at him in horror, I clutched at Prince's bridle. "You're lying," I whispered. He had to be lying. Not even Celeste would be so cruel. Yet even as I thought the words, I knew they were wrong. Celeste would definitely be that underhanded. She didn't care who got hurt in her search for a new husband.

"Go look, wife," Nathan advised. "I suggest you start packing, but don't bother with frills or laces." He looked her up and down, then smirked. "I'll buy those myself."

My stomach roiled and I tightened Prince's girth before climbing into the saddle. Tears burned, clogging my nose as I trotted away. I might tramp about like a farm hand, but Maddy O'Connor didn't run. Not where anyone could see me, at least.

I took a quick detour to the general store for a newspaper. It wasn't an accepted means of courtship, but finding a husband out west was looking like a wiser idea every day. One of the men advertising for a wife had to be a better choice than Nathan Bergman.

Hell, Toby Greer, the shopkeeper's son and barely a day over seventeen would have been a better choice. I tucked the paper into my saddlebag and set off toward Dahlia's farm a few miles north of town. She'd help me choose a man from this very paper.

2

 ALEB

I GRIMACED and tried to bully my mare into good behavior. She spun a few times, nearly unseating me before I got her going in the right direction. Justin had a better hand with our range horses, but even he had trouble with the half-wild stock we'd gathered. We couldn't afford better, or the time to train them. Not that either of us had the interest in the job.

Between caring for two hundred head of cattle, the fence meant to keep them penned, and running them to market, we barely had time to sleep, much less make our shared house into something acceptable for a bride. I wasn't sure what I'd been thinking advertising for a wife, but I did it anyway. The desire for a woman of our own knocked the good sense clean out of my head.

Aside from that, it was almost April. I'd nigh on promised Justin our wife would be here before the weather turned.

Maybe Justin was right, and I'd been dropped on my head as a baby, although I couldn't recall such an incident. I wasn't sure why, but something told me I was doing the right thing with that silly advertisement for a bride.

I decided to let him think I was crazy. We'd both spent too long watching the men of Bridgewater create families with their chosen women. We wanted what they had, a woman to please and care for. More than that, we needed her. We hadn't had a woman between us in months, but I wanted more than a soiled dove. We would fuck her into bliss, and she'd wear the same self-satisfied smile all the Bridgewater ladies wore when they looked at their husbands.

Justin was my best friend, and my brother in all but blood. I didn't give a damn what people thought about his ebony hide, or the wiry curls he kept almost shaved to his scalp. If the woman who answered my ad didn't accept both of us, she could turn right around and get back on the train.

My advertisement would get us a wife. I was sure of it. I couldn't explain the itches of premonition I got sometimes, but they'd never steered me astray. The one time I ignored my gut almost got me leg shackled to a woman who wouldn't accept Justin in my life. Carrie Frye had been my daddy's choice and was presentable enough, but her personality left much to be desired.

I followed Justin as he headed north out of town, his gelding settling into a lope under his gentle hand. When we reached our homestead, carved out of the space between a snowcapped peak and a sheer escarpment leading down into a verdant pasture, we got back to work on the chores we'd ignored in favor of going to town.

I climbed off my horse and grimaced at a section of broken fence. We'd lost nearly a third of our herd in the last few weeks—too many to be a natural predator—and more disappeared every day. Our cattle were gold on the hoof, and the loss irritated me to no end. Hopefully, we weren't looking at a situation with a rustler. People in Bridgewater took care of their own and I'd have heard about it if that was the problem. Regardless of the culprit's identity, we were no closer to finding our missing cows.

I mentally calculated the funds we had left to carry us until our next cattle drive. We'd be able to feed ourselves, but we didn't have much saved up to support a wife. Instead of chewing on the problem, I finished fixing the fence and trusted my gut. The right woman would come, and she wouldn't give two pennies about our finances.

As usual, my mare snapped at me when I made to mount her. I blocked her with an elbow, reminding her of her manners. When I finally gained a seat in the saddle, I scratched her withers in a half-hearted attempt to soothe her. "Be still, sweetheart. Your day is almost done."

She bucked, nearly unseating me. I barked out a laugh and spurred her toward home. The sun was almost below the horizon when I arrived, and my stomach growled. What I wouldn't give for a good steak supper from the hotel in town, but we'd have to make do with boiled beans and burnt biscuits.

Neither of us had ever learned to cook. With luck, our new wife would be able to make fluffy biscuits and juicy roasts, but it wasn't a priority. I wanted a woman who would embrace both of us. She would love Justin as much as she loved me, and we would spend the rest of our lives making her too happy to leave. Despite his misgivings, Justin was as anxious as I was to claim a bride in the manner of Bridgewater grooms.

The thought reminded me I still needed to find a chunk

of hardwood and some free time to carve a plug for our wife's backside. She'd need to be well-prepared for taking both of us. I smiled to myself. We hadn't even seen the woman yet, and I was already thinking of how her lush bottom would squeeze around my cock as we fucked her together.

"What's for supper?" I asked, kicking my boots off at the door. We were both making a concerted effort to keep the cottage tidy in anticipation of our bride's arrival. Once she got here, we'd be too busy making her scream our names to bother with cleaning.

"Same thing as always," Justin replied, handing me a plate. "But I have a surprise for you." He laid a sealed telegram on the table between us. It had been sent from St. Louis, but I didn't know anyone out that way.

"What's this?"

"Ezra Thompson from the mercantile dropped it by while you were taking care of the south fence. I'm hoping it's an answer to our advertisement." His cheeks darkened and he spooned beans to his plate. "I thought we'd read it together since it's addressed to you."

I broke the seal and almost fell out of my chair. "She's coming," I breathed, wiping my mouth with the back of my hand. Lord have mercy, I was almost drooling at the thought of finally getting a wife of our own.

In just a few days, we'd have our woman in our arms. We'd set our every waking moment to ensuring her pleasure, and I couldn't wait to taste her sweet pussy. I wanted her desperate cries in our ears as we saw to her wanton needs.

Handing the thin paper to Justin, I let him read it, wishing I'd taken the time to carve a plug for our new wife. Our fingers would have to do for now. We'd finally get to feel her squeeze our cocks like a vise as we fucked her. At least the big bed we'd share was finished, including a brand-new goose down mattress.

His eyes narrowed. "Arriving on noon train Wednesday in answer to your advert." Laying it on the table, he pointed at the initials on the bottom. "Who's MO?"

"Margaret?"

"Maybe Matilda?"

Laughing, we began our meal. "I suppose we'll find out next week," I replied. "We'll celebrate with these biscuits that aren't burnt to a crisp."

He grunted in acknowledgement, then swallowed his food. "Maybe the mercantile has oranges. Think our new wife might like some?"

The minute he mentioned it, my mouth watered for the crisp citrus and I wondered if our future wife would use lemon soap. Her bare skin would smell like sunshine and taste like the lemon ice my father used to buy for Justin and me when we finished our chores. If she didn't, I'd be sure to buy her some just so I could lick the sweet essence from her delectable pussy.

MADDY

I POCKETED the advertisement I'd torn from the paper. *Wife needed, aged eighteen to thirty-five. Must be able to cook and clean for two healthy men, aged thirty and twenty-nine, owners of JC cattle ranch north of Bridgewater, Montana Territory. Must be willing to work and have a horse and saddle. No portrait necessary.*

I was willing to bet the man I selected, one Caleb Mathis, hadn't gotten any responses. A smart woman would think the man was addled for what he was asking, and wouldn't consider traipsing out west to be a glorified servant. None of his requests bothered me though. I liked to cook, and a tidy household was my preference. Aside from that, he'd specifically mentioned wanting a wife with her own horse. That meant he had ideas, and I wanted to hear them.

Mr. Mathis had to be better than the gentleman who hadn't said anything aside from the desire for his bride to be pretty, along with the words protect and cherish.

Cherished and protected, indeed. All husbands wanted a pretty wife. Mr. Mathis did too, even if he had sufficient wit and manners to resist putting it in a newspaper. Would he not do those things if he didn't consider his bride attractive? How would he feel if his new bride didn't find *him* appealing? I snorted and tucked the rest of the newspaper away, setting aside my curiosity about both men being in the Montana Territory.

I had no interest in spending my days as a pampered pet. Being stuck inside bored me to tears. A man who dared ask his wife for the things in Mr. Mathis's advertisement was looking for a helpmeet—not an ornament he could trot out to impress his equally dull friends.

Tucked in a small purse sewn into my drawers, I had almost a thousand dollars in savings from Prince's stud fees and the pin money Daddy had given me over the years. It would be more than enough to get me to Montana Territory and leave a healthy dowry.

Maybe, just maybe, if God saw fit to answer my prayers, Mr. Mathis would be the one to put that secret smile on my face. If he didn't suit me, his partner might. There was no sense putting all my eggs into one basket, after all. One of them would be the one to show me what it meant to be a woman and a wife.

Dahlia didn't think much of my idea of becoming a mail order bride, but she helped me anyway. I promised to write her the minute I arrived, and to skedaddle back to Kentucky if Mr. Mathis turned out to be unacceptable.

I knew she worried, but something told me Mr. Mathis was just the man I needed. I was strangely excited by the prospect of leaving Kentucky behind and wondered what my future husband looked like. Being a rancher, he likely had big strong hands with calluses. I shivered, imagining his rough palms stroking my tender skin.

But to get to my soon-to-be husband, I had to escape Lockerbury without Nathan or Celeste finding out.

Dried walnut husks turned Prince's pale golden coat into liver chestnut, and some of Reggie's old clothes turned me into a vagabond with an ugly horse. We found an old nosebag to hide Prince's conspicuous appearance.

Dahlia dropped her paintbrush in the empty dye bucket and scowled. "You look horrible," she muttered.

"Perfect." I smoothed Reggie's trousers over my backside. They didn't fit very well, but a little discomfort was a small price to pay for getting Prince to safety. "I'll send Reggie's clothes back when I get settled."

"Take as long as you need. Reggie hasn't worn those in ages and he'll never miss them. Just send me your new address the first chance you get."

"Dahlia! Is supper ready yet? I'm as hungry as a bear, and I want to kiss my beautiful wife."

The sound of Reggie's voice echoed from behind the house and Dahlia winced. "You better get out of here," she whispered.

"Not yet. If Reggie recognizes me, we did all this work for nothing."

Biting her lip, she nodded and turned to wave at her husband. "Reggie, this here fellow says he needs a job. Do you need help with the planting?"

Reggie approached and wrapped his arms around Dahlia, kissing her cheek. He took off his hat, revealing short cropped brown hair turning gray at the temples. "Sure am sorry, but I can't afford to pay for help. You might try the next town over. I hear they're looking for folks to mine coal."

Trying to deepen my voice, I said, "Thank you kindly. I'll be on my way and leave you good folks to your supper."

"You're welcome to break bread with us, stranger. I can't let a man go without a good meal to tide him over," Reggie said.

I dredged up a smile, wishing I could have found a man like Dahlia's husband. Thin and tall like an overgrown beanpole, Reggie wasn't rich or handsome, but he loved his wife to distraction. I wanted that so badly. To my mind, his dedication to Dahlia trumped everything else. "Thank you, but I'll be on my way. I can make the next town before dark."

Dahlia looked like she was about to cry, but nodded and waved as I vaulted up on Prince's bare back. We'd hidden the sidesaddle deep in Reggie's barn, where hopefully it would rot. Dahlia even packed me a small canvas satchel filled with food for the train ride and loaned me a second dress so I'd have something clean to wear when I arrived.

I wasn't sure how to feel about Reggie not recognizing me. He'd known me for years and I didn't like leaving without saying goodbye. Yet it also meant I'd most likely pass through town unchallenged. Tapping my heels to Prince's sides, I urged him into a canter toward the train station.

The fare for us both was a goodly chunk of my savings, but it couldn't be helped. Prince was quiet as the porter loaded him, giving only a soft whicker as he disappeared inside the car.

As the door slid shut behind him, I heard Nathan's husky voice along with the grating sound of Celeste's complaints. Stiffening, I ducked out of sight behind a stack of baled tobacco.

"Did you see her get on the train?" Celeste asked. "She has to be here."

"No," Nathan replied. "I wouldn't miss a pretty redhead in a blue dress riding a palomino. Are you sure she didn't go home? Maybe she's hiding in the barn with that damned horse."

"I'm telling you, she isn't there, and none of her things are gone."

It was rare to see Celeste so flustered, but I didn't have time to enjoy the sight of her red face and less than perfect hair. Keeping my head down, I scurried up the metal steps into the train as the conductor called for boarding. Let them figure it out on their own. I'd be in Montana and hopefully married before they found me. I found a seat next to a man with a heavy satchel and pulled my borrowed coat tight around my body to better hide my appearance. As the whistle blew, I sent up a little prayer that I'd find Caleb Mathis in a good humor, and good skill in bed.

Keeping my movements hidden from my seatmate, I stroked my hands up my thighs under my coat, imagining what his touch would feel like. My belly clenched and I bit back a whimper when the man next to me snorted in his sleep.

The long trip gave me time to think. The second my new husband got me in front of a preacher, he'd be the owner of almost a thousand acres of prime Kentucky bluegrass pasture, lock, stock, and the entire damned barrel.

I was absolutely sure Nathan and Celeste had some scheme worked up to steal my home out from under me. My active imagination spun me all sorts of tales that rang with suspicion. It was possible I was wrong, but I didn't think so. Although the whole story sounded like something out of a Gothic novel, Celeste's underhanded tactics, along with the short few days Nathan had given me made me almost sure those two were up to something nefarious.

When the train stopped in St. Louis, I sent Mr. Mathis a telegram advising him of my arrival. I also decided not to tell him of my bequest. At least, not right away. It was probably the imaginings of a silly little girl, but I wanted the man I married to want me because of me—not because of money.

And if he could give me a secret smile like the one Dahlia always had, I'd count myself doubly blessed.

3

$\mathcal{J}$USTIN

THE NOON TRAIN pulled through town a few minutes after we arrived, disgorging one passenger, a small man in ragged clothes with unkempt brown hair tucked under a battered cap. Unfortunately, no women exited any of the cars.

Biting back my disappointment, I dismounted and jerked my chin toward the stranger. "You think he might need a job? Looks like he might work for bread and board."

Maybe our new wife was busy gathering her things after her trip. It was possible she'd missed a connecting train somewhere too. I doubted our mysterious lady would have bothered with a telegram if she hadn't intended to show up. The thought cheered me a bit, and at the very least, we might be able to convince the small man to work for us.

With extra help, we'd be able to spend more time

preparing for our wife's arrival too. My cock swelled as I thought of finally being able to trace her soft curves and holding her between us.

Caleb grunted, stepping away from his mare when she tried to bite. I had no idea why he insisted on riding the cantankerous beast. Pure stubbornness, I supposed. That was as good an explanation as any.

"Maybe," he finally said. "We could use the help."

Nodding, I dropped my horse's reins over the hitching post and approached the small man, stopping short when a porter led an ugly brown stallion from the train. The horse jerked free and made a beeline for the small man, rubbing his nose against the stranger's chest.

The man let out a surprisingly high-pitched giggle and scratched the stallion's face. He led his horse to the livery stable without bothering with a lead rope, making me wonder if he could take our range horses in hand, especially Caleb's.

"He has a good touch with horses," Caleb murmured, joining me as I leaned against the fence surrounding the livery stable yard.

"With that chestnut stallion, at least." Hopefully, the stranger wouldn't take too long. Clouds, carrying the dry scent of incipient snow, were forming and even Caleb was giving the sky a distrustful glare. Montana weather was unpredictable at best this early into spring. One day might be warm enough to work in shirtsleeves, but the next might produce a foot of snow.

We waited in the stable yard until the stranger returned. As he passed us, I held out a hand, stopping him. "You have a mighty good touch with horses, friend. Are you looking for work? We can offer room and board until we get our cattle sold. If things work out after that, we're willing to talk salary."

Shivering, the man drew his coat tightly around his small frame and lifted his chin, revealing strikingly pale green eyes the color of spring grass. "No, thank you, sir, but perhaps you could help me. I'm looking for Caleb Mathis. Could you direct me to his ranch?"

"You've found him," Caleb replied, taking a step forward. "This is my partner, Justin Carter. What can we do for you?"

The man pulled off his hat, revealing a long swath of oddly colored brown hair. In fact, the hue was a near exact match for the stallion's ugly hide. His voice changing to a higher, decidedly feminine pitch that made my cock twitch inexplicably, he glanced around and said in a voice barely above a whisper, "My name is Madelaine O'Connor. I'm here in response to your advertisement for a wife."

Caleb coughed out a laugh and shook his head. "I'm afraid we're looking for a woman to be our wife, but the offer of a job stands if you're interested."

O'Connor amused me, that was for sure, and it had been a long time since I'd found anything funny. Despite myself, I was interested in the small fellow's story. "What really brings you out to Montana?" I asked.

Gritting his teeth, the man inhaled and let his air out slowly before speaking. "Sirs, will you direct me to the nearest hotel and wait for me? At least give me a chance to prove my gender."

Whoever this Madelaine was, he had nice manners. I couldn't rightly recall if anyone had ever called me sir. That predisposed to me to like him, regardless of his tall tales.

Laughing outright, Caleb nodded and pointed toward the clapboard hotel at the end of the street. "We can give you an hour. After that, we're heading home."

O'Connor grinned impishly, his button nose wrinkling. "I won't need that long. Wait for me in the dining room and I'll buy you supper for your trouble."

Without another word, he walked away, leaving Caleb scratching his head. "What do you think?" he asked, turning to face me.

I watched O'Connor stride toward the hotel, cocking my head at... Was that the sway of a round bottom under a too-often mended coat? It was hard to tell under all that dusty gray fabric, but it made me wonder. "Don't rightly know," I finally said. "Might get us a free supper though."

We followed O'Connor into the hotel, watching with interest as he paid for their best room and asked for a bath. When he had his room key, he turned and said, "I won't be long."

When I nodded, he disappeared up the steps, his boots making no sound on the polished wood floor.

———

CALEB

SOMETHING WAS WRONG HERE. This whole situation set me on edge. Was this O'Connor fellow telling us the truth? I'd never heard tell of a woman dressing as a man, or vice versa. It didn't make much sense to me, and raised a whole mess of questions I wanted answers to.

Namely, how did a person exiting one of the third-class train cars, male or female, have the funds to engage the hotel's best room and buy supper for three, along with a hot bath?

"You're scowling," Justin muttered. "What's on your mind?"

"I don't like this." I shook my head and strode outside. If O'Connor was truly female, she'd take forever making herself presentable. We had plenty of time to discuss our options. I lowered myself into one of the rockers set out on the porch for guests and lit a cigar. "Why would a woman disguise herself as a man? Did you see him pay for the room outright? Where did he get the money?"

"There's that stallion too. He's ugly as sin, but I'm beginning to wonder if O'Connor stole him."

"I don't think so." I took a puff from the cigar and passed it to Justin. "Did you see how the horse followed her? When was the last time you saw that?"

"That old flea-bitten gray plow horse of your daddy's. Remember how he used to follow your mama around?"

Laughing, I retrieved the cigar. "Yep, I sure do remember that. Mama had a right good hand with him too."

Justin leaned back in his chair and crossed his hands over his belly. "So maybe O'Connor didn't steal the chestnut stallion. Doesn't explain why he has so much money."

"No saddle or tack either. Just a rope halter he didn't use." I handed the cigar over.

Justin laughed and took it from me. "He or she?" He took a puff, then stubbed it out. "I'm thinking O'Connor is the woman we're waiting for."

"Why?"

"Madelaine O'Connor. The initials match what was on the telegram. Aside from that, she has an awfully high-pitched voice."

"Still doesn't explain why she's dressed as a man."

My best friend lifted his shoulders in a shrug. "Safety.

Traveling by herself would have been risky for a young lady, and she can't be more than twenty or so."

"True. Pretty manners too."

Nodding, he smiled grudgingly and pulled his hat over his eyes. "I could get used to being called sir, especially if she's on her knees asking for my cock. I'm going to rest my eyes for a spell. Wake me when she shows up."

"He, you mean?" If O'Connor truly was the woman we were waiting for, we'd both get the pleasure of what Justin described. I couldn't help the faint hope welling in my chest that traveled lower into my gut, making my shaft thicken. She sure did have pretty eyes and I couldn't wait to see them clouded with passion.

Well, if she really was a woman, that was.

"Either one."

I nodded and lit another cigar. The clouds were starting to drift apart, taking away the dry scent of snow. Didn't mean it wouldn't snow later, but we could afford to wait a little longer.

Several minutes later, just as my eyes were drifting shut, a graceful feminine hand plucked the cigar from my fingers. I sat up, nearly tipping the rocker backward as I stared up into vivid green eyes surrounded by damp curls the color of a sunset, although a few strands remained a dusty brown.

Madelaine was definitely a woman, and stunningly beautiful in a neat blue cotton dress that hugged a shapely waist and pert breasts I suddenly wanted to suckle. Her tattered coat made me frown. It wasn't suitable for the weather here and barely covered her.

She took a puff off the cigar and handed it back, then gave me a small grin. Lord have mercy, the sight of her in that prim dress made me hard as an iron pipe. I let out a breath, reminding myself no honorable man would take her into the alley, flip her skirts up and fuck her. Her plump lips would look so beautiful wrapped around Justin's shaft.

Justin's chair fell backward as he leaped to his feet, belatedly snatching his hat from his head. His brown eyes wide, he gaped at her like a caught fish. I didn't have to look at the front of his trousers to know he'd be just as hard for her as I was.

The men of Bridgewater always said they just *knew* when the right woman came along, and now I understood what they meant. Madelaine O'Connor was going to be ours. Tonight, she'd be between us in a marriage bed, screaming our names in passion as we made her our wife in truth.

I gazed at her, unable to speak for a moment. All the blood that made my brain function went straight to the hardening shaft in my trousers and I imagined laying her down in our brand-new bed. We would strip her out of that dress, and I would waste no time finding out if she tasted like lemon ice and warm woman. "I, uh..."

"Do I meet your expectations, sirs?" she asked.

My eyebrows went up. "You really did see the advertisement? Came all this way to be our wife?"

She nodded once. "I did."

I stiffened. Our bride traveled alone, disguised and without protection. We wouldn't be allowing that again.

"I've already taken the liberty of ordering supper for the three of us. I hope you don't mind steak." She turned, obviously expecting Justin and me to follow.

I wasn't about to let her get away so easily. I'd have to turn her over my knee and spank her bare bottom pink to get the truth out of her before I did anything else. Catching up with her, I took her arm and pulled her close before she reached the door. Whispering in her ear, I asked, "Why were you dressed as a man, Miss O'Connor?"

Justin took her other arm and loomed over her on the other side. "Why was your hair dyed? Are you running from something?"

"The short answer is yes," she hissed back. "You'll have to wait for the long answer until after the wedding."

"Long answer now," I retorted, needing to know the woman who would be ours was not in danger. "I also want to know where that stallion came from."

"His name is Prince, and I've had him since he was a yearling. He's part of the long story I want to tell you." She shivered in her thin coat. "If you've finished your cigar, may we go inside? It's quite cold."

Biting back a curse, I wrapped an arm around her slim shoulders, hurrying her inside once Justin opened the door. I wasn't about to let her go. Whether she wanted to admit it or not, Madelaine O'Connor would be our wife before the sun set. After that, we'd show her what it meant to be a Bridgewater bride. My balls ached with anticipation, and I wanted to take her straight to the small church. After we loved her to sensual bliss, we'd feed her from her hands until she was sated with delight.

Her footsteps slowed as we approached the Franklin stove and she held her hands over its heat, rubbing them together. "I think you have a long story to tell me too," she murmured softly.

"Oh? What do you mean?" I asked.

"Why do you say *we* and *us* when you're talking about looking for a woman to be your wife?"

Rubbing my face, I gave her a shamefaced grin. As usual, I was putting the cart before the horse, but I was too anxious to get her into bed where she belonged. "I suppose you're right, Miss Madelaine. Are you ready for supper?"

"It depends," she replied, her eyes twinkling with amusement. "Are you going to tell me your long story in exchange for mine?"

"Of course. Afterward, we'll answer all your questions."

"Thank you." She bit her lip and looked toward the restaurant. "I do owe you both an apology. I'd intended to present myself at your ranch in proper clothing after a bath and a good night's sleep. I can well understand how my appearance must have confused you at first, but it was necessary."

Her immediate apology mollified me, but I was definitely going to spend some time with Madelaine O'Connor turned over my knee. She was too independent and willful by half and would probably spend quite a bit of time with a reddened bottom in the future.

"I'm sure that's part of your long story," I murmured.

"It is. Shall we go in to supper? I've already paid for it, so we might as well enjoy it while we tell each other our stories."

I bit my tongue against the questions that raised. Where had she gotten money for the train passage and the hotel, plus a steak dinner for three people? There weren't too many ways a woman could earn money, and she didn't look the type to make a living on her back. It made me wonder as to her safety. A rich woman having to disguise herself to get away?

I held my curiosity in check, unwilling to offend her. Besides, we hadn't figured out she was a woman until she'd appeared in a dress. We'd been so busy on the ranch, we probably couldn't pick a soiled dove out of a pack of church ladies. We had a bride now and had to be more attentive.

Holding out an elbow for her, I asked, "Shall we, Miss O'Connor?" When she nodded and laid slim fingers on my arm, I leaned close, inhaling the scent of lemon soap, just as I'd imagined. I couldn't wait to get our future wife between us. We'd have her begging for the passion only Justin and I could provide.

4

M ADDY

JUSTIN LAID his coat around my shoulders, wrapping me in warm wool that smelled like bay rum and spices. I inhaled deeply and smiled up into his handsome face. His cheeks darkened with a blush and lowering his head, he cleared his throat.

"Are you warmed up?" he asked.

"We're inside now." I tried to return his coat, but he wrapped it firmly around me.

"You can give it back when you stop shivering."

He was frankly beautiful, with high cheekbones and warm ebony skin. His brown eyes were soft and kind, especially after I apologized for my unintentional charade. Although he was at least a foot taller than me and huge with hard muscle, he made me feel safe instead of afraid.

I met his gaze and my breath stalled in my throat. Something hot and itchy took up residence in my belly and my core dampened with sudden need. I shivered, but not because of the frigid weather.

"Let's get you to supper before you catch cold," he murmured. "We'll ask for a table next to the fireplace."

"Thank you." I allowed him to put his arm around me, and resisted the urge to burrow against his warmth. Caleb took up a position on my other side, lending his body heat as well. I was fair chilled from the bitter spring wind swirling through town. It seemed I hadn't been truly warm in days. I hadn't realized how cold it would be this far west and had only Reggie's old coat to protect myself from the elements.

Caleb Mathis wasn't conventionally handsome, but I found him ruggedly appealing. He was unkempt, with several days' growth of dark blond beard on his jaw, and had icy blue eyes. He smelled, but I didn't find his scent unpleasant. Instead of perfumes and pomades, he smelled of pine, warm horse, and healthy man.

He seemed every bit as protective as Justin. Being between them was... comfortable. I wondered if Prince would like them. I was more willing to trust my horse's judgment than my own. The touch of their warm hands was exactly as I imagined it would be, although I never imagined having *two* men touch me. Hard and rough, but strangely gentle at the same time. My nipples pebbled and rasped against the bodice of my dress, making me ache inside. Their hands on me...

Oh, I couldn't want both of them! It simply wasn't done. Yet the thought persisted, and I couldn't shake my imaginings of what it would be like for both of them to touch me with their work-roughened hands.

"Do you have a private room with a fireplace?" Caleb asked the waiter, dragging me from my thoughts as we stepped into the restaurant.

The man brightened as he looked up, giving us a welcoming smile. "Hello, Caleb. Haven't seen you in here since last fall. Good to see you as well, Justin."

"Been busy on the ranch. It's calving season."

"Good luck with it. Turning into a right nice year for the Bridgewater herds." Turning to grin at Maddy, he asked, "And who is this pretty lady?"

His hand tightening on her fingers, Caleb said, "If we can remember how to court a lady, she's gonna be our wife."

Our wife? I shook my head, sure I'd misheard. It wasn't the first time one of them had said something like that though. The thought of having them both sent another sharp thrill through my belly, but it wasn't possible. The law had an ugly word for someone who took more than the bible said they could.

"Congratulations, and welcome to Bridgewater, Miss..."

"Riordan," I replied, pinching Caleb's hand as I gave the waiter my mother's maiden name. "Thank you."

"Where do you hail from, Miss Riordan? We don't get too many ladies from back east."

"Illinois," I lied, hoping he wouldn't catch my soft drawl. It was bad enough that silly dye hadn't lasted through one washing. I didn't need my stepmother or Nathan asking questions about a redhead from Kentucky. "I've just arrived today."

Caleb glanced down at me, his expression stiff and angry as the waiter led us through a door into a small dining room. He helped me into chair and stood next to me until the door shut behind the departing waiter.

Both men loomed over me, trapping me with their larger bodies. Caleb pinched my chin between his fingers and said,

"Explain yourself, Madelaine. I don't tolerate liars, and I'm about to turn you over my knee and take my belt to you."

Justin looked disappointed and I hated knowing I was the one who put that expression on his face. Caleb just scared the spit from me. I didn't think he was kidding about his belt.

I bit my lip, tears welling in my eyes. I knew how this must look, and it wasn't fair of me to keep things from the man who might soon be my husband. "I'm sorry. It wasn't my intent to lie to you."

"What did you intend?" Caleb asked. He sat next to me, his face softening. "Sweetheart, what are you afraid of?"

"We're not going to hurt you, Madelaine, but you have to tell us the truth before we can help you," Justin said, sitting in the chair on my other side.

The tension in my shoulders eased and I let out a breath I hadn't realized I'd been holding. They looked so earnest and caring, I couldn't help trusting them. Both men would make fine husbands for any woman.

"My name is Madelaine O'Connor, Maddy to people I like. My mother's maiden name was Riordan. I'm from Kentucky."

"All right, honey, tell us the rest," Caleb ordered.

"My mother passed when I was a child, and my father remarried a horrible woman named Celeste. He died several months ago, and Celeste decided she wanted to remarry, but needed to get rid of me first."

"Get rid of?" Justin asked, frowning. "Did she hurt you?"

I chose not to share the scarred lines across my backside from Celeste's cane. "No woman wants a young stepdaughter around while they're courting. She decided to marry me off to the saloon keeper, but he waters his bourbon, cheats at cards, and he has...ladies in his upstairs rooms. I don't like him. He makes me physically ill."

Justin shared a glance with Caleb, then said, "I see."

"And to convince me to go along with it, she sold Prince to him. He said if I didn't marry him, he'd send Prince to a slaughterhouse."

Caleb scratched at his beard and scowled. "He's just a horse. What makes him so special?"

Jerking away, I stood and went to stand by the fireplace, letting the glowing coals send welcome heat into my body. "My father gave him to me, and he's my best friend. You may not care, but I do. He's also valuable. All his foals have grown into outstanding saddle horses."

"Horses are free for the trouble of rounding them up," he countered. "Can't see why anyone would buy one. Where did you get the money to come out here?"

"His stud fees, and what I managed to save from my pin money over the years. Maybe he isn't valuable out here, but he's mine and I'm not going to let some slimy saloon keeper kill him out of spite or because my nasty stepmother wants me gone."

He didn't answer, and I returned to sit across from the two men. "That's why Prince and I both need to stay hidden. Nathan and Celeste might look for us, but I doubt they'll come this far. And once I marry, my name will change and Madelaine O'Connor won't exist to be found."

The door opened, revealing the waiter with a heavy tray. I shut my mouth and gave him a soft smile of thanks as he laid out our meals. When he left, I checked the door before laying a napkin in my lap.

"I suppose you need to get married quickly then. It's not going to do you any good to stay in this hotel," Caleb said. "The preacher will marry us after we eat."

"Does that mean you forgive me for lying?"

Justin shrugged and gave me a shamefaced grin. "Well, we were insulting and rude to start, and fibbed a bit too. We can cook and clean for ourselves, so we don't want a woman to wait on us hand and foot. It seems to me you're only missing a saddle you don't really need."

"Then why did you ask for it?" I took a bite of overcooked green beans, grimacing at the wilted vegetables. If this was what they considered good cooking, I wouldn't be hard pressed to improve on it. Although Justin and Caleb seemed happy enough with the meal, the beef was overdone and tasted like shoe leather.

Finishing up his steak in a few quick bites, he said, "We wanted a strong woman with enough good sense to survive out here without coddling." Pointing his fork at me, he added, "And any woman who can disguise herself and a horse, then travel halfway across the country to marry two men she doesn't know must have more gumption than most of the menfolk around here."

My lips twitched into a grin. "Why, Mr. Carter, I believe you just paid me a compliment."

––––––

JUSTIN

"It won't hurt our feelings if you're willing to cook though," Caleb said. "Neither of us have any skill at it."

"I like to cook," she replied, her eyes sparkling with mischief. "Just wait until you taste my biscuits."

Maddy O'Connor sure was beautiful when she smiled. Her green eyes lightened into a shade that reminded me once more of spring grass, and that pretty bowed mouth looked just right for kissing. In an effort to stop staring at her, I turned my attention back to my meal, surprised when I found it gone.

I took her hand and kissed her knuckles. Our future wife was fascinating, and the more I learned about her, the more certain I became she was the exact woman we'd been praying for. I had to admit some attraction to her even when I thought she was a man. Maybe those tall tales told by Bridgewater grooms about knowing their wives at first sight had some truth to them.

"We'd be most thankful if you took over the chore," Caleb replied. "Justin's biscuits are like burnt rocks."

"We'll be good husbands for you," I said, ignoring Caleb's words. "We might not be rich, but you'll want for nothing, and no wife will ever be so cherished."

Her brow wrinkled, making me want to pleasure her until the frown disappeared. She would be delicious and I couldn't wait to taste her sweet pussy.

"I think it's time I hear your long story now. Will you please tell me why you both say *we* when you're talking about a wedding? It sounds as if you expect me to marry both of you, but that's quite impossible."

Clearing my throat, I took a sip from my water glass and scowled at Caleb for leaving me stuck with the explanations. He smirked and ate the last bite of his cornbread, swirling it through the juice left from his green beans. We weren't ashamed of our desire to share a wife, but we knew outsiders would judge the families of Bridgewater harshly for their choices.

"Well..." I took a sip of water to give myself time to think. "Bridgewater is a special place, and things here are a little different than you might be used to."

"How so?"

"It all started in a place called Mohamir."

The skin between her brows smoothed. "That's near Egypt, if I'm recalling it correctly. Did you and Caleb fight in the war there?"

I blinked, then nearly burst out laughing at the shocked expression on Caleb's face. It appeared our new wife had a rather broad education.

"How did you know that?" Caleb asked.

"My father and I used to study geography together. He was a professor at Kentucky University." Her pretty face fell slightly at the mention of what was obviously a fond recollection. "We'd sit on the veranda and share a cigar and sip bourbon while we talked about all the places we'd like to visit someday. I wanted to see the pyramids."

If her father had allowed it, I couldn't rightly fuss at her for drinking and smoking, especially if she associated it with such a pleasurable memory. Instead, I nodded in understanding. "We did not, but several of Bridgewater's men were there. Maybe you can talk to them one day."

"Yes, please." She clasped her hands together, nearly bouncing in her chair. "That would be wonderful. I've never been anywhere, you see."

Reaching over, I tapped her nose. "That is an outright fib. You've been almost all the way across the United States."

Maddy blinked, then blushed a charming pink. "Yes, I suppose that's true. I don't know why it didn't occur to me. Will you tell me what Mohamir has to do with Bridgewater?"

"There are certain customs in Mohamir regarding marriage," I began, trying to decide how best to explain it. "You see, women are highly prized in that country, and to keep them safe, men... Well, that is to say—"

"A woman has two husbands there," Maddy interrupted. "They believe it's the best way to protect her should something happen to..." Her voice trailed off and her eyes widened. "You've brought the practice here. How is that possible?"

"It wasn't us, but Justin and I want to embrace the Mohamiran ways. One of us will marry you legally, but you'll be wife to both of us," Caleb said. "We will both be fathers to your children."

"Our lives will be spent making you safe, comfortable, and happy. That is, if you accept us," I added, shooting Caleb a dark look. He was bound and determined to claim her. So was I, but I wasn't about to drag her to the preacher and force her to make her vows.

Not yet, at least. I wasn't above using the tease of the sensual delights we could bring her to further our cause.

———

CALEB

She stood and walked to the window, her back to us. Justin laid a hand on my shoulder when I made to go to her. "Give her a moment," he whispered.

Although I wanted nothing more than to pull her into my arms and give her all the delight we could offer her, Justin was right. I nodded and bided my time while she made up her mind about us.

"Does this mean I don't have to choose between you?"

"Yes, Maddy," I said gently. "You'll have us both, and we'll devote our lives to making you happy."

I swallowed the other words I wanted to say. I wanted to

tell her how we'd pleasure her. How no inch of her body would go untouched when we claimed her, and how she'd know nothing but joy for the rest of her days.

"Which one of you will be my legal husband?"

I shared a look with Justin, then said, "We've decided to let you choose."

"Very well. Will you tell me about your ranch?"

Wishing she'd turn around, I said, "It's about five miles north of town, and we have a house already built. You're welcome to decorate it as you like after we get our cattle to market."

"It goes without saying you have a house. I'd like to think you aren't sleeping in your barn or outside."

The amusement in her words made me smile and I almost teased her about spying on us. "All right. What did you want to know?"

She turned to face us, revealing a wrinkle of worry between arched brows. "I was more interested in your stock counts, acreage, whether you have a stable water source, hired hands, and if I can expect a reasonable level of autonomy while I decide where my skills will be most useful."

I gave her the information she wanted, pleased when it made her smile. In fact, she looked positively delighted, even though we didn't have much. I wondered if she'd have that same cheerful smile after we made love to her.

Justin took her hand and kissed her knuckles. "You don't need to work, honey. We'd never ask you to. The only thing you have to do is be safe and comfortable."

Maddy's eyes tightened in irritation. "I'm not accustomed to idleness. Aside from that, you're attempting to manage two hundred head of cattle during calving season without any hired help. You can't afford to push me off to the side."

I shared a look with Justin. It went against everything we believed to allow her to do ranch work. It was back-breaking labor and could be dangerous. I didn't even much care for the idea of her cooking for us, but only a foolish man would turn down her offer. Maybe this was one of those times we'd need to pick our battles. If industry kept her happy, then we could give her that.

Of course, if Justin and I did our part correctly, she'd be too exhausted from our loving every night to get up to mischief. My cock swelled and I smiled, knowing Justin and I would begin the important duty right after our wedding.

"All right, tell us what you think you can do."

She rested her palms on the table. "I can maintain fence, and I've spent some time with cattle, though I don't claim to be an expert hand with them. I can also manage your horses and get them trained to the point you won't have to fight with an unbroken range horse. I can take a few of your better mares and get them into foal with Prince so you can see what a good horse is worth. Give me leave to do whatever I think I can. Be patient with me when I make mistakes, and let me help you. If you give me those things, I'll marry you."

We nodded, accepting her terms. "Have you finished eating?" I asked, frowning at her barely touched plate.

"Yes, thank you. I suppose we ought to go to the church before it gets much later."

"Not yet," Justin said. "First, while you'll be bride to both of us, you have to choose which of us you'll legally marry."

ᴹⁿ ADDY

Sᴏᴜᴇᴇᴢɪɴɢ me between them after that fateful coin toss, Justin and Caleb escorted me from the room. I could barely walk by myself. How could a body feel so much pleasure and still remain conscious? I tingled all over. Was this what Dahlia felt like with Reggie? No wonder she smiled all the time. Oh, and they'd touched me like that in a hotel restaurant! Although we had a private dining room, sound carried. If word ever got out I'd never bear the shame of it. Then again, my two men were just about to be my husbands, and a woman ought to obey.

The thought made me feel somewhat better, but I'd have to make sure not to incite them again, at least not when we were out in public.

"Caleb and Justin!" a woman's voice called. "Come, join us and introduce us to your bride!"

My face flamed at the smiling gazes of a threesome at a

table positioned far too close. Judging by their smiles, they'd heard everything. I tried to hide behind Justin's massive form, but he wasn't having it and kept me locked against his side, pressed tightly between his hard body and Caleb's.

Their cheerful grins weren't cruel though. All three wore expressions of genuine delight. Two men surrounded a young blonde woman with flushed cheeks and a look of supreme satisfaction with her lot in life. All were finely dressed, and appeared comfortably well off. The woman wore a pale green dress, revealing a slim, yet well-proportioned figure, while the men were very handsome in warm woolen shirts and dark trousers.

"Robert, Andrew," Caleb said, nodding to each man in turn. "And Miz Ann. How are you this fine evening?"

"Very well, thank you. Will you introduce us to your new wife?" Robert asked.

"This is Miss Maddy. We're headed to the church right now," Justin said.

Andrew arched a brow, his expression darkening. "Ann, love, will you take Maddy and help her freshen up? Robert and I need to have a few words with Caleb and Justin."

I scanned the men's faces, disliking Andrew's judgmental glare. Lifting my chin, I returned his ferocious scowl with interest and wriggled free to stand in front of Caleb and Justin. "Is there a problem?" I asked tartly.

Both Andrew and Robert blinked at me in surprise, but Ann giggled and rose to her feet. "I'll take you to the powder room," she said, rounding the table. "Robert and Andrew want to yell at your new husbands for a bit to make sure they haven't besmirched your honor."

Robert nodded, peering at me speculatively over the rim of a teacup.

"Oh? What happens if I besmirched theirs?"

Tea sprayed from Robert's mouth and he choked as Andrew pounded his back. Ann let out a tinkling laugh and dragged me away. "You and I are going to be the best of friends, I just know it."

"Lord help us all," I heard Andrew mutter behind us.

Extricating my hand from Ann's tight grip, I patted my hot cheeks as she led me into a small powder room. A tiny oil lamp provided scant illumination, revealing a vanity table and a somewhat cloudy mirror. "I have no idea what made me say such a thing. Please, accept my apologies for causing a scene."

"Don't worry. You're absolutely perfect." She beamed and encouraged me to sit on the low stool at the vanity, then pulled a few pins from her coiffure. "We'll get your hair presentable for a wedding, but we'll need flowers, and... Let's see, you have a blue dress, so that just leaves something new, something old, and something borrowed. Did they tell you the story of Mohamir and how Bridgewater came to be?"

"Yes, I'd heard of Mohamir before, but it's all quite fascinating. I hope to talk to some of the men who were there."

"My Robert and Andrew will be most pleased to tell you what they saw. They spent some years in Mohamir and Egypt."

"Will your husbands be very upset with Caleb and Justin?" I asked, chewing on a thumbnail as Ann twisted my curls into order.

"No, of course not. It's...well, honor is very important to the men of Bridgewater. It's just not done for men to take liberties with their wife before the wedding."

"But they didn't. I mean, obviously you heard, but... Well, they didn't." Ann's words sent warmth deep into my chest. Justin and Caleb could have had their way with me as a husband should take his wife. Their wife, I silently corrected myself. I was so muddled with delight, I'd have let them without question. Even though their need was obvious, they'd controlled themselves for my benefit.

The remembered feel of Justin's thick member rubbing against me sent a fresh surge of wet heat through my tender womanhood and I shifted uncomfortably on the cushioned stool. My nipples perked into tight, achy buds as I recalled Caleb baring me to his avid perusal.

A few hot tears pricked my eyes, and I thanked God for giving me that newspaper all those weeks ago. I even thanked Nathan and Celeste for showing me the way to Bridgewater and my two wonderful men. I was growing to trust them more with each passing minute, and I'd be able to tell them about my bequest soon. Yet the thought made me frown. Would Justin and Caleb be accepted in Kentucky? It wasn't likely, and I couldn't ask them to leave their home either. They'd made a life for themselves here. I resolved to think about it later.

Ann nodded knowingly and dusted a bit of powder across my nose. "I thought it was something like that. The most important question is, did you like it?"

"How could I not? It was..." I tried to find words for the surfeit of sensation my men had given me, and their solicitous care. "It was...astonishing."

"Well, then everything will be fine. Let's get back to what's important." She unclasped a strand of white pearls at her throat and wrapped it around my neck. "Here's something borrowed. What should we do for something old and new?"

"My boots are old, but I don't have anything new, I'm afraid."

"Hmm." Ann put her hands on her hips and cocked her head. Her face brightening, she said, "I know. Those hairpins are new. I just got them last week. I believe that satisfies everything."

I rose and gave Ann a brief one-armed hug. "Thank you. It's good to find a friend so soon after my arrival."

"How long have you been here?" she asked.

"I arrived today on the noon train in response to Caleb and Justin's advertisement for a wife."

"Oh, goodness! You must be exhausted! How far did you come?"

"I..." Biting my lip, I decided to tell the truth. I was sure I was safe enough to be honest with my new friend. Well, at least I would be once Caleb married me. "Kentucky. My stepmother wanted me gone and colluded with a horrible man to force me to marry him, so I had to escape."

She patted my hand in commiseration. "You're quite brave. Andrew and Robert also saved me from a most unwanted marriage, but I'd have been too frightened to make my own way as you did." Grimacing, she added, "Of course, I was on a ship at the time, so escape was quite impossible unless I wanted to swim."

"I think I'd have taken my chances with the sea monsters before marrying Nathan Bergman," I muttered, still shuddering at the thought of that despicable man laying a hand on me. "My stepmother sold my horse to him, and he threatened to send him to slaughter if I didn't agree."

"How awful for you." She hugged me again, smelling of sweet lily of the valley. "We'll get you safely married, and you'll never have to worry about that horrible man or your stepmother ever again. I am sorry about your horse though."

I grinned and rose to my feet. "Don't be. My friend

Dahlia and I painted him brown with walnut dye. I dressed as a man and got us both on the train with no one the wiser."

Giggling, she clapped her hands together. "That's utterly brilliant! I can't wait to tell my husbands your tale. I almost wish I'd been that clever and brave, but then I might have missed Robert and Andrew."

"I hope they find it more amusing than Justin and Caleb did. They were quite upset with me. I'd planned to make myself presentable and ride out to their ranch, but they were the people I asked for directions when I arrived. I didn't mean to tell them a falsehood."

The thought made my stomach tighten around the unpalatable meal I'd tried to choke down. What would they say about my bequest? I had to tell them soon.

"I'm sure they've already forgiven you."

Straightening my spine, I nodded, resolving to forget all about Kentucky— at least for the time being. "Will you stand with me?"

Ann flashed me a brilliant smile. "Of course! How could I refuse my new friend?"

———

JUSTIN

"Tell us about your new bride," Robert ordered, clearing his throat after choking on Maddy's parting shot across his bow. Despite his years out of the military, he'd never quite lost the air of command. Andrew was no better in that regard, but I supposed we owed them an explanation. He was right to ask.

Good men simply didn't debauch a woman without having put a ring on her finger first. Although I was sure he and Andrew had both enjoyed soiled doves in the past, as had Caleb and I, we'd never countenance it without their express consent. We'd been too eager with Maddy, but she was too tempting to resist.

I wanted to see her eyes cloud with passion again. I needed to taste her more than I needed to breathe, and my body demanded I make her mine. In an effort to hide my thickening cock, I sat down across the table from them. Caleb joined me a few seconds later, suffering the same condition.

"She's...unusual, to be sure," Andrew murmured. "You'll have a time bringing that one to heel."

"Hold your tongue," Caleb snapped. "I'll not listen to you disparage our wife."

"She's not your wife," Robert replied, giving us a smirk I wanted to punch from his face. "Perhaps we should introduce her—"

When Caleb growled, I held up my hands in an attempt to stop the coming fight. As much as I wanted to beat Robert to a pulp, it wouldn't be helpful, and I refused to stand in front of God with Maddy after fighting. It was disrespectful and I wouldn't sully her special day with violence.

"Enough," I said, my voice deepening with implied threat. "You two are the only reason we're not at the church right now. Maddy is perfect just the way she is, and we won't hear a word against her."

Caleb settled, but shot a dark look at Robert and Andrew. "She came all the way from Kentucky dressed as a man in response to my advertisement for a wife."

To my surprise, reluctant appreciation crossed Robert's face. "Why was she in men's clothes?"

I told him the rest of her adventure, my chest swelling with pride at his exclamation of admiration.

"Clever," Andrew murmured. "That was incredibly foolhardy."

"But brave of her," Robert said, nodding. "Why is the horse so important that she'd go so far?"

"She says he's valuable," I replied. "She had enough funds from his stud fees to get here on the train, rent the hotel's finest room, and pay for our supper."

"He's supposedly an Arabian," Caleb added. "He's about sixteen hands, and very distinctive."

"Small ears and a concave face with large nostrils?" Andrew asked, leaning forward with interest.

"Yes. How did you—"

"Three dollars a mare for stud services," he interrupted. "Present the deal to your Maddy. I'll go as high as five. Ten if he's native-bred."

"She says he's from Morocco," I replied. "The beast follows her like a puppy."

A dreamy smile crossed his features, softening the harsh lines of his face. "Robert, do you remember the mares we had in Egypt?"

Nodding, Robert said, "Yes, fine animals they were. I would have liked to bring them back with us."

"Make it fifteen. I won't insult Maddy with less." Coughing, Andrew flushed, then added, "Your new wife has brought you two lucky bastards a fine dowry."

"I don't give a damn about her dowry," I replied, my fists clenching at the look of avarice on Andrew's face.

"The horse doesn't matter to us, aside from being something Maddy loves," Caleb added. "We don't care about money. She's what's important."

"Ten dollars is acceptable, sir. I don't plan to overcharge

my new neighbors," Maddy said, surprising me into stillness by plopping herself into my lap. Wrapping an arm around my shoulders, she kissed my cheek. "I'm delighted to see a man who knows his horseflesh out here in the wild mountains."

"Would you be interested in selling—"

The smile fell from her face, making Andrew lean back warily. "Not under any circumstances," she said firmly, rising to her feet. "He's mine, and so are Caleb and Justin. If you'll excuse us, we're on our way to a wedding."

Robert blinked, then shared a telling glance with Andrew. "Of course, Miss Maddy. We'll escort you and bear witness to this happy event. Welcome to Bridgewater."

"Madelaine, if you please," she retorted.

Caleb barked out a laugh and I lowered my face to hide my grin of satisfaction. I liked being claimed by Maddy, but sooner or later, he and I would have to teach her she could relax and let us protect her instead of the other way around.

I wrapped my coat around Maddy's slim form before we left. It was much too cold for her in that thin cotton dress. We'd have to buy her a more appropriate wardrobe soon. She couldn't have much money left after getting herself here, and once she was our wife, we would take care of her needs.

We sandwiched her between us, Caleb on her left while I took my position on her right as we escorted her down the street to the church. Her soft curves felt perfect in my arms. I couldn't wait for the wedding to be done. I wanted to take her back to the hotel and finish what we'd started in the restaurant.

Robert and Andrew followed with their Ann snugged up between them.

As usual, the church door was unlocked, but we'd

probably have to search for the preacher. Likely, he was in the parsonage with his wife, seeing as how it was suppertime and the sun was setting.

Maddy's feet stalled and she looked up at the white clapboard steeple, biting her lip. "Are you ready, sweetheart?" I asked, leaning down to inhale the fragrance of citrusy soap.

She jumped and gave me a tremulous smile. "Yes, of course. Shall we?"

Keeping a firm hold on her waist, we escorted her inside.

———

CALEB

"Do you have a ring?" the preacher asked. "I can sell you one for two dollars if you don't, and you can pay me back when you get your cows sold."

"I think I have it, but that's awful kind of you," I replied, praying I had that much. Digging into my pockets, I scowled when I produced no more than two bits. I didn't bother to look to Justin for the dollar fifty we needed. He never carried money. I fumbled a coin and bit back a curse when it hit the wood floor.

Dropping to her knees, Maddy bent down and shifted her weight, hiding her movements. A second later, she stood and handed me two silver dollars.

"These fell from your pocket. You need a coin pouch." Letting her lips curl into a smile, she reached up and kissed my cheek. "I declare, I'd lose every single penny I had if I didn't have one."

I gritted my teeth, unsure whether to thank her or take

her outside for a sound spanking. Where on earth did she get that money? It didn't escape my attention that she'd essentially paid for a ring she hadn't wanted in the first place. Infernal woman.

I barely listened to the thankfully brief ceremony. There were only a few words I wanted to hear.

"I now pronounce you husbands and wife. You may both kiss your bride."

She lifted her chin, pursing her lips as her eyes closed. Cupping her cheeks in my palms, I kissed her gently, and not quite chastely. Her lips parted and my cock surged in my trousers when she let out a little gasp of air. I took full advantage, deepening our kiss until she whimpered softly. Before she could catch her breath, I passed her to Justin and grinned when her knees buckled under his expert touch. Our new wife was a passionate thing under that prim blue dress.

The sound of the preacher clearing his throat pulled us out of the spell Maddy cast upon us with her soft lips. He handed us a hastily prepared marriage certificate. Folding it carefully, I put it in my pocket for safekeeping.

We made our goodbyes and left the church. Maddy hissed out a breath as snowflakes dusted her face, and Justin wrapped his coat more tightly around her shoulders.

"Let's go back to the hotel," he murmured, pulling her into his arms to share his warmth. "It's too late to go home tonight, Mrs. Mathis."

Her teeth chattering, she scowled up at the sky. "It's almost April! How c-can it be snowing in April?"

"We'll see about getting you a good coat tomorrow," I promised.

"Yes, please. I had no idea it would be so cold."

It wasn't that bad, but if I recalled correctly, Kentucky

was a bit more temperate than Montana. When her blood thickened up, she'd be fine. We hurried her down the street, her small frame nestled against us.

I let her sit by the Franklin stove while Justin took care of our horses. Not a moment too soon, we had her upstairs where we could warm her properly—with her naked body between ours.

Justin unlocked the door and lit an oil lamp, revealing a spotless chamber. The bed was more than large enough for all three of us and covered with a patchwork quilt. A wooden dressing screen stood in a corner, and there was even a chamber pot tucked discreetly under the bed. The washstand had a full pitcher of water, and several snowy white towels in a neat stack. A small table rested in the center of the room, surrounded by three chairs. This hotel was well prepared for Bridgewater families.

The shutters were tightly closed against the weather, and a fire was already laid, waiting to be lit. Setting her down on the bed, I knelt in front of the hearth and soon had a small blaze going to warm the room.

Maddy sat on the edge of the bed and twisted her fingers together. "I don't even have a pretty nightgown to impress my new husbands."

"Do you want one?" I asked as Justin locked the door. She didn't seem the type to crave fripperies, but we barely knew her.

She turned to look at me, her eyes glowing in the faint lamplight as she stroked the coverlet on the bed. "Not really. Seems a waste to spend money on something I'll wear only once." Grinning impishly, she added, "I wouldn't say no to a glass of good bourbon if such a thing is available out here."

Justin laughed softly and shook his head, then walked toward her on bare feet. "I'm afraid it's too cold for bourbon and a cigar on the veranda. Aside from that, it's time for us to make you our wife in truth."

A pretty blush colored her cheeks pink and she blinked up at him. "How? I mean, there are two of you."

I tipped her chin up for a kiss. "We're going to show you, sweetheart, but we're going to have a little chat first."

6

M ADDY

MY BELLY SWIRLED and I wondered if I was about to need that chamber pot. Had he guessed my secret? Oh, heavens! What if Nathan and Celeste had found me? I needed Caleb to make me his wife in truth. The thought of Celeste trying to force an annulment was unbearable. Daddy's will said her permission wasn't required for me to marry, but I didn't trust her.

"I..." I swallowed hard and willed my hands to stop shaking. "What did you want to talk about?"

"Why did you pay for that wedding ring when you didn't want it in the first place?" Kneeling, he unlaced my boots, his strong fingers making quick work of the chore before sliding them from my feet.

The breath left my body on a relieved sigh. Although I'd have to tell my husbands the truth sooner or later, I didn't want to do it tonight. "I have no idea what you're talking about, Caleb Mathis. I did no such thing. You dropped that money on your own accord, and I just picked it up."

Chuckling, Caleb sat on the bed next to me and hauled me over his lap. "A lady shouldn't lie," he advised as he let his hand fall smartly to my upturned bottom.

I shrieked and tried to wriggle away, kicking my feet. Shifting his weight, he captured my flailing legs between his calves and started spanking me in earnest. The thin fabric of my dress was no protection against his punishing hand, and I felt the bulge below his belt buckle swell and press against my hip. He swatted my bottom several more times, roasting my tender flesh.

"Stop it!" I cried. "Ouch!"

My protests didn't carry much heat. Although his spanks stung a bit, warmth trickled into places it had no business going. I pressed my thighs together and bit back a moan of pleasure. I couldn't understand why a spanking made me feel like that, but it did. My womanly parts softened and grew damp, making me swallow a whine.

"We're going to make sure you don't lie to us again, Maddy," Justin said.

Caleb spanked me again and I screeched as I tried to cover my bottom. He caught my wrists gently and held them at the small of my back. "It's Justin's turn now. We're going to redden your backside very well so the lesson sticks."

Justin yanked my skirt free and tugged it over my hips, then pulled my drawers apart. Crying out, I struggled harder, knowing they could see my private shame.

Caleb's hand stilled, resting on the curve of my bottom, and Justin let out a sharp hiss. "Who did this to you, Maddy?" Justin demanded, lifting me from Caleb's lap.

He sat me on the bed between them, my skirt still hiked around my hips. My head spun at the sudden movement, but I pressed my lips together and looked away. "It's nothing. It happened a long time ago."

"That's not what we asked," Caleb replied. "Who whipped you hard enough to make you scar? Aside from that, some of these are new. It wasn't your father, was it?"

"No! He would never!"

"Your stepmother, then." Justin wrapped his long arms around me, pulling me to his chest. "Too bad she's a lady."

I sniffed and looked down, unwilling to see the pity in their eyes as they each took one of my hands. "Why is that?"

"If she was a man, Caleb and I would go to Kentucky and give her a sound thrashing. Might do her some good to get a taste of her own medicine."

Imagining my husbands doing just that made me smile and I risked a peek up at them. "I'm sorry I told a fib."

"Aw, honey." Caleb embraced me from the other side and both my husbands cocooned me in their comforting warmth.

Although my bottom ached, my husbands hadn't done me any real harm. Celeste had done much more damage with that stupid rattan cane of hers, and she hadn't stroked my flesh to ease the sting. Not that I would have accepted comfort from that horrible woman.

The news about my bequest was on the tip of my tongue and it needed to come out, but I couldn't let anything else spoil our wedding night. I resolved to wait and tell them when we had plenty of time to talk about it, and after I'd fed them a good meal to sweeten their dispositions.

Justin tightened his arm around me and wiped at a few tears with the pad of his thumb. "We aren't mad that you did it, honey, but we're not going to let you lie about it. Are you gonna tell any more lies?"

They held my hands too tightly for me to cross my

fingers behind my back, so I crossed my toes instead. "No, sir."

"That's our good girl," Caleb murmured. "We're proud of you."

His words nearly made me lose control of my emotions. I hadn't heard anything like them in months, and it made me feel even worse about not telling them my secret. I wiped away a few fresh tears and laughed softly. "I have no idea why I even said such a ridiculous thing. You're a grown man and had to know how much money you had in your pocket."

"I know it was less than two dollars, and I didn't have anything larger than a nickel."

I nodded and bit my lip. "I didn't want you to lose face in front of the preacher and I thought if I pretended it was your money, it would have all been forgotten." I squirmed, trying to figure out why my bottom was still warm when the spanking was over. I wanted to rub at it, but judging by the way it felt when I shifted my weight, it would make things worse instead of better. It was a most discomfiting sensation. "I just wanted everyone to be happy," I added.

Justin grunted in acknowledgement and nodded. "That's a fine thing to wish for, sweetheart, but you don't need to lie to get it." He tipped my chin up with a gentle finger. "Understand?"

"Yes, sir."

He smiled, straight white teeth gleaming in the dim light, and pulled me into his lap. "That's my good girl," he crooned. Lowering his lips to mine, he kissed me softly.

I sure did like it when my husbands kissed me. I couldn't believe I had to come all the way out to Montana to find a man who would kiss me the way I liked. Caleb and Justin were both so gentle and careful with me. I truly did feel like I was the most important thing in their world.

Of course, I'd never been kissed by anyone before, but that didn't seem to matter overmuch when Justin moved to the spot under my ear I hadn't realized was so sensitive. His lips were warm and so damned soft as he brushed my skin with sucking little kisses that made me quiver under his touch. Delicious tingles coursed down my spine as I shifted restlessly on his lap. The fabric of his trousers abraded my tender backside, making me achy and restless and I wrapped my hand around the back of his neck to drag him closer.

Chuckling softly, he pulled away and I whimpered in disappointment. Helping me to my feet, he stood and stroked my shoulders, his fingers falling to the buttons of my dress. His brown eyes met mine, so warm and soft, and he said, "Are you ready to be our wife in truth, Maddy?"

My throat closed and I swallowed the growing lump, then nodded.

"We are too," Caleb said. He helped Justin with my dress, and added, "We sure are glad you came out west, sweetheart."

"Me too." I shivered as my bodice fell open, revealing my body to their avid gazes. Part of me thought I should be scared, but I wasn't. Their looks of longing made me feel cherished. Caleb unfastened my skirt, allowing it to fall to the floor while Justin untied my drawers. I winced when my money pouch made a soft tinkling sound against the floorboards.

"Your nest egg, I presume," Caleb said, picking it up.

"Yes. I—"

Without a word, he nodded and dropped it into my boot.

"Whatever you have left after traveling here is still your nest egg. We'll provide for your needs from now on."

I blinked and nodded dumbly. He hadn't even opened it. Did he truly care so little about money? That was...almost incomprehensible. Yet it meant he and Justin wanted me for me, and not for what I could bring them. Suddenly, I didn't give a tinker's damn about my bequest. I'd arrange with Daddy's attorney, Mr. Fuller, to have it sold because I wasn't going back to Kentucky.

My heart nearly burst with adoration for them. I reached up to undo the buttons on Caleb's shirt. Bulging muscles appeared under my fingers and I held back a gasp as I pushed the heavy cotton off his shoulders. Lightly furred, his chest was a mass of muscle, matched only by his heavy arms. Crisp dark blond hair narrowed to a trail leading into his trousers, and I traced it with a wondering finger as the ridges of his abdomen rippled under my touch.

Turning to face Justin, I did the same, each button I released allowing a tantalizing glimpse of his smooth bare skin. He was every bit as muscular as Caleb, perhaps even more so, for he was quite a bit larger in stature. My breath caught as they laid gentle hands on me, petting my shoulders soothingly.

"You haven't had a man before, have you?" Caleb asked, his hands stilling on my arms. "We don't care overmuch if you have, but we want to know if we need to be especially gentle."

I arched a brow and grabbed my dress from the floor, suddenly too shy to speak with them while I wasn't dressed. "I'd likely have married him if I had." Remembering my shift and corset had been left behind with my sidesaddle, I asked, "Do I seem like a fallen woman to you?"

He kissed my forehead and gave me a wry grin. "No, but you do seem like a woman who goes after what she wants."

"I suppose that's true enough," I agreed. "But that's one thing I've never wanted, until now." I let the dress fall to my feet.

Caleb drew in a breath and stepped back, wiping at the stubble on his face with a shaking hand. "Lord almighty, you're beautiful, Maddy Mathis. We must be the luckiest men in Montana."

The compliment, obviously heartfelt, made heat rise in my cheeks. My father, and even a few other men with courting on their minds, had called me pretty, but no one had ever called me that and meant it. It made my heart positively melt in my chest.

"Let me see you," I whispered.

"Not yet." His blue eyes glittered as he took my hand and led me to the bed. "It's my turn first." Still wearing his trousers, he dropped to his knees in front of me as Justin pushed me gently to the bed, then climbed up behind me.

"What are you doing?"

"Making you ready for us." He put his hands on my hips and pulled me forward, then buried his face between my legs.

I cried out in surprise, then rested my hands on his shoulders as he pushed my thighs apart and licked my most private place. Growling, he used his thumbs to open my woman's flesh and sucked the nub at the top of my sex into his mouth. My core spasmed, and my hips bucked at the overwhelming pleasure he delivered. How had I never known such a thing was possible?

I bit back a hysterical laugh. Maybe that was why Dahlia always looked so happy in the morning. Justin held me up, his large hands covering my breasts as he kissed my neck.

Softening his mouth, Caleb eased a finger into my untried channel. I bit my lip at the slight sting, and it vanished when he swirled his tongue around the sensitive bundle of nerves. Something twisted and tightened in my belly as he pushed his finger deeper, and my legs shook as I struggled, reaching for something just out of my grasp.

I'd touched myself before, and had even managed to make myself feel good under the covers after the house was asleep. But no amount of exploring or illicit fondling could have prepared me for what Caleb was doing with his mouth and hands.

I pushed my fingers into his hair, gripping the silky strands tightly as I bit back a whine. "Caleb, please," I whispered. "I need something."

He climbed to his feet and loomed over me as Justin stripped the coverlet away to reveal white sheets. Pushing gently on my shoulders, he said, "Lie down and we'll give you what you need, sweet girl."

Legs still quivering, I obeyed, my eyes wide as he shucked off his trousers, revealing his thick manhood. I'd never seen a man fully naked before, and my breath caught at how beautiful he was. Rampant and hard, the crown of his member glistened with white droplets of moisture. He smelled musky and a little salty, but it wasn't unpleasant, and I inhaled his warm aroma, drawing it deep into my lungs as he stood over me.

I reached for him, pouting when he pushed my hands to the sheets. "Not yet," he murmured. "If I let you touch me, I'm gonna come before I get inside you."

Spreading me wide with his thumbs, he lowered his face to my core and circled my nub with his tongue, teasing me until I bucked against him. He lapped at me, then pushed his tongue inside my channel, fucking me like he would soon do with his hard shaft.

Not to be left out, Justin took one of my nipples in his mouth, laving the tender bud with his tongue before sucking it hard. A jolt of pleasure traveled into my belly.

"Oh, heavens!" I couldn't help my cry of delight. Everything felt so wonderful. Clutching at the sheets, my body quivered as Caleb eased a finger into me once more, stretching my untried opening. Although it stung just a bit, the slight pinch of pain soon faded under his careful ministrations.

I let out another breathless cry as he fucked me gently, carefully adding a second finger as he nipped the turgid bud and licked it to soothe the sting. My channel clamped down on his fingers, the muscles sucking him deeper.

"Caleb!"

He growled his approval as my inner walls fluttered against his fingers. My breath coming in tearing gasps, I exploded for him, my cries ringing in the chilly room as my body raged with the force of my climax.

"That's my girl," he murmured against my flesh. I went limp, my body twitching as he gentled me, soothing my wet pussy with gentle kisses.

"Heavens," I whispered. "That was...I didn't know such a thing was possible."

He moved up my body, stroking me with soft fingers. "We're not done yet, sweetheart. We're just getting started."

7

Justin

I fisted my rigid cock, squeezing hard to keep myself from spilling in my trousers. It had been a long time since we'd had a woman, and Maddy wasn't some soiled dove we could use without thought. She was our wife, and it was our job to take care of her and make her happy.

But she wasn't making it easy. Her little hands wandered, stroking my chest and across my hard nipples, the teasing touches making me insane with wanting her. Yet I let her explore and learn my body, knowing it would make her more comfortable with me. I wasn't a small man in any dimension, and almost wished I hadn't lost the coin toss.

Caleb and I had decided long ago who would take our wife first. We'd planned to let our woman choose who she married legally, and the other of us would be first to bed her. I'd never thought about it much, but looking down at our wife's small frame and untouched body, I worried I'd be too big for her.

Maddy shifted, bending her knee as she dragged a finger down my chest. "I thought you said we weren't done," she whispered, putting her lips to my chest. She trailed soft kisses across my belly, then moved up to bite my nipple.

My cock surged, threatening to burst through my buttons. "Naughty girls who bite might get their bottoms spanked," I warned.

Remembering the scars crisscrossing her lovely bottom, I wanted to take the words back the minute they flew from my mouth, but she laughed.

"Maybe naughty husbands ought to get on with making their wives feel good," she retorted, tugging my head down to kiss me. Letting me go, she kissed Caleb as well, her hand dropping to play with my belt buckle.

She was so playful. I wanted her to keep that joy forever. We would keep her safe and innocent for as long as we lived.

I let her push her tongue into my mouth, then sucked it gently as I swallowed her whimpers of pleasure. She smelled so damned good, and I thanked all the heavens I'd talked Caleb into helping me heat water for bathing before coming into town. Now that we had our Maddy, I didn't see him complaining about the chore again.

Pulling away, I cupped her face and stared into her pretty green eyes. "Are you ready for us?" I asked. "It's likely to hurt some."

Maddy blinked once and nodded, her expression growing somber with apprehension. "I'm ready. I want this."

"We'll be as gentle as we can," I promised, standing for just long enough to take off my trousers.

Her eyes widened and she bit her lip. Lying next to her

Caleb stroked her hair, gentling her nerves. "Do you trust us to be careful?" he asked.

"Yes," she said, after taking another long look at me. "I know you won't hurt me."

I settled myself between her slim thighs, careful not to crush her, then positioned myself at her entrance. Carefully and almost too slowly, I eased the head of my cock inside her, watching her face for any sign of discomfort. "Relax, honey. Let me inside so I can make you feel good," I crooned.

She let out a slow breath, and her body softened for me, still silky and damp from Caleb's ministrations. Pushing forward another few inches, I waited until she breathed again.

Instead of relaxing as I expected, she lifted her hips, taking me the rest of the way inside her, then let out a soft cry as her eyes shut tight.

"I'm sorry. I promise it will only hurt this one time, Maddy."

She wrapped her arms around my neck and pulled me close. "I know, and I trust you. You're going to make it better for me."

Her words humbled me, and I was more determined than ever to give our new wife passion like she'd never dreamed. I rocked my hips slowly, giving her a chance to adjust to my size. This couldn't be easy for her.

Taking one of her hands, I pushed it between our bodies and laid it over her sensitive nub. "Use your fingers to make yourself feel good," I murmured. "I want you to come all over my cock."

Her hand shifted between us and I felt her little fingers move over her tender flesh, "Kiss me again, please," she begged.

71

I'd likely never stop kissing her, but she needed more. As her fingers worked her swollen flesh, I experimented with my movements, watching her reactions to see what she preferred.

Maddy let out a soft cry and her head fell backward as I lifted her thigh and helped her wrap it around my waist, allowing me to go even deeper. "Do you like that?" I asked.

"More, please?"

I settled into the slow rhythm she wanted, my cock surging as her muscles clenched and rippled around me. Lowering my head, I nipped at the sweet spot under her ear, then trailed soft kisses down the side of her neck, licking at her silky skin as she shuddered. My balls tightened and I slowed my movements, desperate to make her come before I let go.

Making love to our new wife was like heaven and I never wanted to stop. Her sweet perfume made me forget all about the ranch, broken fence, and missing calves.

I hissed at the sting of her sharp nails digging into my shoulders, her fingers tightening as her pussy gripped my cock like she'd never let go. Her skin flushed pink with exertion and I kissed the wrinkle between her eyes, my hands roaming down her flanks as I made love to our wife.

She tightened her leg around my hips, driving me faster as her desperate whines goaded me. Her fingers worked furiously between us and the slick gush of her pleasure tempted me into tasting her as Caleb had. My balls ached and swelled, and I whispered, "Come for me, sweetheart. Let me feel you come on my cock."

"Don't close your eyes, darling," Caleb admonished. "Watch Justin fuck that beautiful pussy." He reached between our straining bodies, pressing down on Maddy's fingers. "See how wet you are for us?"

Letting out a sharp scream, her eyes widened as she spasmed around me. I fucked her harder, desperate to bury myself so deeply inside her she never doubted for a moment the passion between us.

"Justin! I'm going to—"

"Let go, honey," I encouraged, resting my forehead against hers. Her pretty eyes were cloudy with desire, and I kissed her parted lips, tasting her with soft flicks of my tongue as she kissed me back.

She spasmed, digging harder into my shoulder as she froze. Her channel sucked at me and I thrust into her one last time as my balls tightened. She rippled around me, and I let out a hoarse shout as she dragged me into climax with her.

Maddy wrapped her arms around my shoulders as I collapsed on top of her, my heart thundering in my chest. Although I was almost too spent to move, I rolled off her and pulled her into a tight embrace. Kissing the top of her head, I whispered, "That was mighty fine, Mrs. Mathis. Mighty fine, indeed. Are you ready for more?"

―――――

CALEB

"Such a good girl," I murmured, brushing a few strands of damp red hair out of her face. "You took that big cock so beautifully. We're proud of you."

"This is where you'll sleep," Justin said. "Between us so we can pleasure you at will."

"And you'll never be cold," I added.

"Mmm. I'm not cold now," she replied burrowing her face in Justin's chest.

I laughed softly and rolled to my back. "Come here, darling. You're going to ride me."

Maddy rolled over and peered at me, her face still flushed with passion. "I don't understand what that means."

"So innocent and sweet," Justin said. "You're going to straddle his hips and fuck him."

"I don't believe that's how things work." Maddy bit her lip, looking so adorably confused I wanted to kiss her.

"Have we led you astray yet?" I tossed an arm over my head and stroked my cock, rubbing my thumb over the plum colored crown as precum dribbled from the slit. Her eyes locked on my shaft and I hid a smile when she licked her lips. I couldn't wait to see that sweet rosebud mouth wrapped around my cock. "Have we done anything you haven't liked?"

"Yes. Supper was awful."

Justin and I chuckled. We both thought the food was fine, but it must not have been up to her standards. Maybe there was a little bit of pampered eastern princess in our bride.

"Up you go," Justin said, helping her to her knees. "Look at that sweet pussy, all swollen and ready for another good fucking."

Her cheeks turned bright red and she threw her hands over her face. Despite her obvious embarrassment, a trickle of fresh moisture leaked down her thigh. Justin swiped a finger through it and sucked it into his mouth.

"You taste delicious, Miss Maddy. Now, climb on Caleb."

"You are both naughty," she muttered. Yet she did as we asked, tossing a knee over my hips to straddle me awkwardly. "Like this?"

"Almost." Justin got behind her and eased her knees farther apart until her core touched me.

I hissed out a breath, desperate to control myself. "That's a good girl, Maddy." I stroked the silky red curls guarding her womanhood, making her hum in pleasure as I lined my shaft up with her opening.

"Lower yourself on him," Justin encouraged. "Take his cock inside you."

Biting her lip, she stared down at me, obviously nervous and unsure but so willing to please us. She sank down on me, and closed her eyes as I filled her. Whimpering softly, her head fell back against Justin's chest.

"Such a good girl," he crooned, teasing her nipples into stiff points. "Move on him. Make yourself feel good."

"I don't know—"

I put my hands on her hips, helping her rock back and forth on my cock as I encouraged her with short thrusts into her hot cunny. "Like that, darling. Show us how you like to be fucked."

"Oh, oh! My goodness!" Leaning forward, she put her hands on my chest. Her hips circled, driving me to madness as she took her delight from my body.

Glancing over her head, I nodded at Justin. It was time to start preparing Maddy for both of us.

Swiping a finger through the moisture trickling down her thigh, he shifted his weight behind her. Her eyes widened and her channel clenched almost hard enough to hurt, telling me the exact moment he penetrated her crinkled rosebud.

"Justin!" Her shriek echoed and I pulled her to me, kissing her to swallow her cries. There no sense disturbing the other guests.

"We're going to take you here," he murmured. "In the

same way Mohamiran wives accept their husbands. We'll fill you with our seed, and you'll know such pleasure from us."

"No," she whined. "That can't be right. It's—"

"You like Justin's finger in your bottom, don't you?" I asked. "I can feel you clench on me. Aside from that, as long as you feel good and enjoy it, nothing between husbands and their wife is wrong."

Justin winked and brushed her hair aside, then kissed the back of her neck. "You said you wanted to learn about Mohamiran customs, did you not? Well, this is most definitely one of them, but you won't be learning it from anyone but us. No one else touches you."

A flicker of indecision crossed her features as I felt him push a second finger into her bottom. She shivered, squeezing my cock. Holding her hips, I surged upward, thrusting inside her.

"We only wish to bring you delight, sweetheart," I murmured, fucking her steadily. Letting go with one hand, I pushed it between our bodies to tweak her sensitive pearl. "Will you let us?"

"I..." Her eyes fell closed and she let out a squeak when I pinched her clit gently. "Oh, God, yes."

"That's our good girl. We want you to come again for us. Show us your passion."

The perfume of her arousal filled the room, making me wish I could bottle the rich, decadent fragrance.

"Please, fuck me."

Her pleading cry along with that delightfully profane word, made my balls draw up. I wasn't going to last. It had been too long since we'd had a woman, but Maddy was well worth the wait. "Come for us, sweetheart," I urged, rubbing her clit firmly as Justin fucked her bottom with his fingers.

Jerking hard, she arched her back and shuddered, crying

her joy as her delicious cunny milked the seed from my cock in spurts. Groaning in pleasure, I pulled her into my arms as Justin stroked her back soothingly and whispered sweet words of adoration into her ear.

"Let's get you cleaned up," he said softly, tucking a piece of hair behind her ear. Her coiffure had come loose, scattering pins everywhere.

When she didn't answer, I frowned and tipped up her chin, then chuckled. "She's out cold."

"Poor thing." He eased her off my chest and into bed. I wouldn't have minded her using me for a pillow, but we needed to bathe her. "She must be exhausted."

I nodded, rising from the bed, then went to the washstand for a damp cloth. "At least ten days on the train, plus meeting us. It's no wonder she passed out."

"Maybe longer," Justin said.

She grumbled softly while we cleaned her, then drifted into repose, her plump lips parted. Carefully covering her with the quilt, we settled into bed next to her, one on either side. Just as it should be.

Justin fell asleep, his face buried in Maddy's hair, and I smiled. My intuition never steered me wrong. Our wife was perfect.

$\mathcal{M}$ADDY

IT WAS lovely to be so warm when a furious snowstorm raged outside. Rolling over, I snuggled into a warm male chest without opening my eyes. Judging by the lack of hair, it was Justin. With the heat of their bodies, I'd likely never need to light a fire again.

His chest rumbled under me with his soft laugh. "It's time to wake up, Maddy. Caleb is fetching breakfast, and you've been out for almost twelve hours."

I shot up out of bed and stumbled over my boots as I grabbed my dress. Stepping into it, I fastened the buttons as quick as I could. "Mercy! Why did you let me sleep so long?"

My drawers were gone, and judging by the happy smirk on Justin's face, I wouldn't be getting them back.

"You appeared to have needed it, what with running halfway across the country and having a wedding night."

I blushed with the memory of their possession of me,

lowering my face to hide it. Justin chuckled and swung his long legs over the edge of the bed, his dark skin gleaming in the early morning sun. His cock stirred under my avid gaze and I whirled around before he caught me peeking.

"Look your fill, sweetheart." The floor creaked under his weight as he moved toward me and laid a gentle hand on my shoulder, turning me to face him. "You're our wife now."

Justin was so beautiful. He looked like a sculptor's model come to life before my eyes. Leaning closer, I tipped up my chin for a kiss. My stomach chose that very moment to give a loud, growling reminder that I hadn't had a proper meal in days.

He frowned and backed away. "You must be starving," he said, pulling his trousers over his hips. "You barely touched your supper."

I laid a hand on my abdomen, flushing anew with mortification. "Sorry. I promise, I'm fine."

He tapped my nose sternly, but smiled. "You'll eat a good meal. After breakfast, we'll take you to the mercantile for some warm clothes, then we'll head home."

The door opened, revealing Caleb with a large covered tray. My mouth watered and I hurried forward to help him. Waving me away, he set our breakfast on the table and removed the cloth.

There was tableware and a carafe of coffee, plus huge bowls of biscuits, steaming gravy, bacon, and a pile of scrambled eggs I was sure we wouldn't be able to finish. My belly rumbled again, making Caleb chuckle.

"Sit and eat, Maddy. Let's soothe that monster trying to escape your stomach."

My cheeks hot, I obeyed and waited while he served me a plate before making two more for himself and Justin. The eggs were fluffy and had just the right amount of salt. The biscuits were as tender and flaky as I could make, and the gravy had the perfect scattering of pepper for seasoning.

Swallowing, I reached for another piece of crisp bacon. "How is this breakfast so lovely when supper was so awful?"

"I found out they had a new cook last night," Caleb replied. "We thought it was fine, but you weren't the only one to complain."

Glancing down at my empty plate, Justin asked, "Are you finished eating? There's still another biscuit if you want it."

"Yes, thank you. I'll burst if I eat another bite." I touched my lips with my napkin, then asked, "Are we ready to go to the mercantile? I also want to check on Prince. He's not used to the weather here either."

"Of course. Put on your boots and we'll head out," Caleb said.

I pushed my foot into my boot, grimacing when I felt the wad of money lodged in the toe. Pulling it out, I handed it to Caleb. "Here, this is the last of my dowry. Will you put it in the bank for me?"

Caleb was on me in a flash, followed by Justin. Pinching my chin, he gently lifted my face up. "We told you we would take care of your needs. That money is yours to do with as you see fit, but you will not use it on us, understand?"

"But I—"

Justin stole my words with a deep, thoroughly drugging kiss, laying me back until I was gasping for air and sprawled on the bed, my bodice half undone. He tugged my hair, making me look at him and Caleb.

"Enough, Maddy," he said sternly. "We'll put that money away for a rainy day. It makes us happy to know you have something to fall back on."

My eyes filled with tears and I nodded. How had I gotten so lucky to have two such wonderful men? It seemed almost sinful when most ladies were lucky if they got one. Or none, I reminded myself, thinking of Nathan Bergman.

"Shh, sweetheart," Caleb murmured, helping me sit up. "We've got you now."

"I know." I leaned against his chest and scrubbed the tears from my eyes, then fixed my bodice. "We should go."

"Good idea," Justin said, helping me to my feet while Caleb packed my meagre belongings. "Otherwise we might be tempted to bed our beautiful wife again."

My blush returned, heating my cheeks as they helped me with my ragged coat. We went downstairs, me tucked between them. When we reached the landing, I blinked in surprise at the sight of Ann and her husbands waiting with a large satchel. Robert held a heavy coat over one arm.

"Oh, good," Ann said, smiling at us. "We were afraid we missed you."

"Were we supposed to meet you for breakfast?" Caleb asked. "I'm afraid we've already eaten."

"No, but we got home and realized your Maddy might need some things to hold her over. The mercantile is a little short on warm clothes this late in the season." Andrew replied, handing the bag to Caleb.

Robert gave the coat to Justin, who helped me exchange it for Reggie's. It fit perfectly, making me realize it must have been Ann's. "Are you sure you don't need this?" I asked, biting my lip.

She waved me away and shook her head. "No, it'll warm up soon enough, and I'm used to the weather. I won't need it for months, so you can use it until then."

"Thank you so much," I murmured, packing Reggie's coat with the rest of my things. "You're very generous."

"We help each other in Bridgewater. You can return the favor for someone else after you get settled."

I nodded in understanding. "Thank you again."

We said our goodbyes and made our way to the livery for our horses. The snow, so furious the night before, was nearly gone from the wooden sidewalks and although still cold, it was a gorgeous morning. I scanned the street, trying to get my bearings, and spotted a post office barely a hundred feet away. Pointing at it, I asked, "May we stop? I'd like to mail something back to Kentucky."

"Of course," Caleb said. "What are you mailing?"

"I need to send Reggie his clothes back."

"Who's Reggie?" Justin asked, his voice deepening to a low, jealous growl that made my insides quiver with renewed need. I reminded myself not to provoke them in public again. I wasn't sure I'd ever get over the embarrassment of being caught by Robert, Andrew, and Ann.

"My friend Dahlia's husband. She gave them to me so I could escape. I'd also like to write her a note to tell her my news."

I couldn't tell her all of it, of course. She'd be appalled and scandalized at the thought of marrying two men—no matter how wonderful they were. It seemed almost disrespectful not to share both my men, but I'd have to keep it to myself. It wasn't as if I'd be going back for her to meet them.

"Ah, she's the one who helped you dye your horse, right?"

"Yes. We're very close, and I promised to send her my address when I arrived."

The postmistress was happy to help us package Reggie's belongings, and I quickly penned a short note advising Dahlia of my new address. I left out everything that might worry her, and simply told her how happy I was. With that chore done, we returned to the livery stable and retrieved our horses.

I led Prince from his stall, belatedly remembering his bridle was gone. It must have gotten left on the train, and I'd been too preoccupied to notice it was missing. I didn't need it overmuch, so I resolved to replace it later. Surely, Caleb and Justin had one I could use.

———

JUSTIN

As USUAL, our horses fought us, and I scowled when Maddy led her stallion from his stall without fuss or a lead rope. When she laughed and came to help, I waved her away.

"Stay back before you get hurt," I ordered, struggling to saddle my gelding.

Maddy nodded, but when Caleb's mare tried to bite, she strode into the fray and grabbed her nose before she could reach his arm. "No," she said softly, looking into the mare's face. "We don't bite."

The mare snorted and lifted her head, but kept her eyes fixed on our wife. A moment later, she relaxed and allowed Maddy to stroke her face. "That's a good girl," she crooned. "Behave now."

"Unnatural," I muttered, finally getting my girth tightened on my recalcitrant gelding before attaching the satchel filled with Maddy's borrowed clothes to the back of the saddle. As usual, the horse danced out of reach when I tried to mount.

"No," she replied, taking my horse's head. She spoke to him in a singsong murmur, making him still and focus on her. "Anyone can calm a horse. You just need to have the right tone."

When I was finally in the saddle, she returned to her stallion and made a strange gesture with her hand. To our shock, the animal lowered himself to his front knees, allowing Maddy to climb on as pretty as you please, her skirts arranged to cover her legs. She let out a short chirp and the horse stood. He barely looked twice at Caleb's mare.

Scowling at her, Caleb shook his head. "Justin is right. That's fair unnatural. Where's your bridle?"

"I think it must have gotten left on the train," she replied. "But I don't need it. Shall we go home?"

"Maddy, you need a bridle," he said sternly. "It's bad enough you don't have a saddle. Why don't you sit in the hotel while I run home and get tack for you?"

I almost offered to let her ride double with me, but I didn't trust either of our horses to carry her safely.

She let out a sigh and shook her head. "I'm truly fine. I'll rummage your barn for tack later. Will that suit you?"

"Let's let her do as she likes," I murmured to Caleb. "We'll put a rope on the stallion and lead him. When we get her home, we can teach her to mind us better."

I had no intention of using physical punishment on our wife, but I was more than happy to deny her physical delight until she obeyed us. Heat rose in my loins at the idea of keeping her dripping and needy until she learned not to be so danged willful.

"Too late." He pointed up the street heading north out of town. Maddy was already trotting away, using her hands and feet to guide her horse as neat as anything.

I chuckled and shook my head. She'd managed to escape while I'd been thinking of how she looked while we fucked her. "Well, we wanted someone who had a good hand with horses."

To my surprise, our horses didn't fight us and seemed happy to follow her. Aside from that, we got to watch her pretty bottom all the way home. We had plans for that backside. Sensing my inattention, my horse danced a jig, reminding me to keep my mind on business.

When we reached the ranch, my chest eased as she passed under the wooden sign marking our property. We'd gotten her home safely, but I still worried she wouldn't like it. She was a fine lady, despite her initial appearance as a man, and had obviously come from money, something Caleb and I didn't have in great abundance.

She dismounted and smiled as she gazed at the snowcapped peaks in the distance, framed in azure blue sky. "It's beautiful here," she said quietly. "Almost like a painting."

Although the day had warmed, she shivered as we led our horses to the pasture and turned them loose. "Are you ready to go inside?" I asked.

"Yes, please. I hope it warms up soon."

"You'll get used to it," Caleb promised, wrapping an arm around her shoulders.

We took her inside and I hung her coat on the hook next to mine, then knelt to unlace her boots. She looked around, and Caleb and I both let out a sigh of relief when she didn't immediately communicate her displeasure.

Her stockinged feet made no sound as she walked across the kitchen to the pantry. "Do you have something besides beans and flour?" she asked.

"We have coffee and salt," Caleb said.

"Oh. Well, I suppose it's too cold for a kitchen garden, but surely you have eggs and milk."

I glanced at Caleb, then shook my head. "I'm afraid we'll have to make do until our next trip into town."

Her face fell and she gave us a pleading look. "But—"

"No," Caleb said sternly. "We'll go another time."

A mutinous expression crossed her face and she pouted, but turned to the pantry and poured beans into a bowl to soak, then filled another with flour and water and covered it with a plate.

"What's that for?" Caleb asked.

"It will be sourdough in a few days. It's the best I can do without proper staples." She wiped her hands on a tea towel, then faced us. "What should we do now?"

I shared a look with Caleb, then we turned our smiles upon our new wife.

9

ALEB

"I BELIEVE it's time for us to show you the bedroom." I said, pulling her to me. Justin loomed behind her and made quick work of the buttons on her bodice, baring her lovely breasts.

"But it's daylight!" she squeaked, turning pink. I adored making our pretty wife blush.

"All the better to see you, darling," Justin murmured, tugging the pins from her hair. It curled down her back in a river of sunset. I'd have to heat up water after supper so we could wash the last bit of dark dye from the flaming tresses.

I slid her dress down her arms, kissing her soft shoulders as it fell to the floor, leaving her clad only in her stockings. Her nipples budded in the chilly air and I bent to suck one into my mouth. She tasted delicious.

"Oh!" Maddy arched her back, her hand coming to rest on my head.

Justin took the other one and stroked a large hand down her belly to her succulent pussy, delving between her folds. She cried out again and pushed her hips forward, chasing the delight he offered. Without warning, he pulled his hand away, making her whimper in disappointment.

"Let's move this to our bedroom," he said. "It's broad daylight, after all."

Without giving her a chance to respond, I swung her into my arms and carried her through the simple wooden door dividing the kitchen from our sleeping area.

Small and cozy, it boasted little more than a fireplace, a washstand and our new marriage bed with a matching night table.

I laid her on the bed, and Justin and I took a few seconds to simply look at her. She was so beautiful and sweet. And she was ours.

Rolling to her side, she propped herself up on a pillow, a teasing smile on her lips. "It hardly seems fair I'm the only one naked. I want to see you too."

I groaned and unbuttoned my shirt. Buttons popped free of Justin's as he stripped it away and his belt hit the floor with a thud. Laughing, she climbed out of bed and gathered the scattered buttons.

"Careful, gentlemen. Sewing isn't one of my gifts," she said, looking up at us. A naughty gleam lit her green eyes and she set the buttons on the nightstand, then knelt at our feet.

"What are you doing?" Justin asked, moving to help her from the floor.

She brushed his hands away, then rose up to open his trousers. "I want to try something."

Cupping his hard shaft, she slid his foreskin back with her thumbs and suckled him into her mouth, his thickness disappearing between her pink lips. Pulling away, she licked droplets of silky fluid away from the purple crown like it was horehound candy.

His head fell back as he hissed a heartfelt curse between clenched teeth. "Oh, fuck, Maddy," he breathed. "You don't...Oh, God."

Our wife was certainly a naughty thing. I crouched next to her and tangled my hand in her hair. "Such a clever girl," I murmured. "Look up into Justin's face and see how much pleasure you're giving him."

Her hair clenched in my fist, I held her head still while he thrust into her sweet mouth. Veins popped in his arms and he stroked her cheek as he gazed adoringly into her eyes.

"You look beautiful sucking that thick cock. Do you like having him fuck your mouth, darling?"

Maddy whined, making Justin's hips jerk. Looking down, I smirked when she moved her hand between her legs.

I let her play for a few moments, just long enough for wetness to slick her folds, then said, "Oh, naughty, naughty girl. That's *our* pussy."

"And you touched it without permission," Justin added, his voice thick and husky. "Hands behind your back, sweetheart."

Whimpering, she obeyed, her eyes clouded with desire and abject need. I took her wrists in one hand, still holding her hair with the other. "That's our good girl," I crooned. "Let Justin fuck your sweet mouth and spray his seed all over those gorgeous tits."

My best friend shuddered, sweat beading his face as he shot me a scowl. I grinned, knowing my filthy words were driving him to the edge. Maddy moaned around his shaft, her hips moving as I denied her what she most needed.

Letting out a shout, he jerked away and fisted his throbbing cock as he erupted, coating our Maddy's chest with ribbons of cum. Panting softly, Maddy leaned against me, a triumphant smile on her face.

"Sweet wife," Justin whispered, lifting her to her feet. "Such a good girl. I think Caleb needs your attentions now, don't you?"

Still smiling, she said, "Why yes, I believe he does."

He led her to the bed and positioned her on her hands and knees. "You're needy and wet for us too, aren't you?" he asked, stroking a hand down her flank. "Such wonderful cock sucking deserves a reward."

"What's my reward?"

"We're going to pleasure you until you pass out again," I replied. "We'll wake you in time for supper."

She tried to scowl, but couldn't quite erase her amusement. "A proper husband wouldn't have mentioned how I fell asleep last night."

Justin knelt behind her and swatted her bottom gently, making her hiss out a breath. Her eyes darkened and she licked her lips, dragging a groan from my throat. Maybe playful spanks weren't completely out. I made a note to remember her passionate reaction for later.

"A proper husband will make you do it every night," he murmured, pushing his hand between her thighs. "I believe Caleb would like the pleasure of your pretty mouth now."

"I've never been one to refuse an invitation," I replied, pushing my trousers open. My cock ached to be inside her and I winced at the throbbing pressure in my balls.

Parting her lips, she accepted me into her mouth and looked up into my eyes when I groaned softly. Maddy's lips were like heaven. Instead of holding her still, I let her play while Justin petted her soaked pussy.

I loved how easy and willing she was with us. It was almost as if we'd known her forever when it had been scant hours.

"You'll take both of us soon, Maddy," Justin whispered, kissing a path down her spine. "We're going to prepare your bottom hole until you can take us without injury."

She let out a low whimper, sucking harder on my cock. Her tongue moved against my shaft, making my balls tighten with need. Crying out, she shuddered, her hips writhing as Justin teased her.

"Do you like my fingers in your bottom, sweetheart?" he asked. "I love how you clench on them, and I can't wait to see what it feels like around my cock."

"Would you come with something in your ass?" I asked, brushing hair from her eyes. "I think we should find out."

"I'll try three fingers," Justin replied. "I'll wager I can make her come."

Her eyes widened and she choked out a whine. Her back hollowed as she thrust her bottom in the air, allowing me to see what Justin was doing. "Oh, that's gorgeous, darling," I crooned. "Look at him, fucking your bottom with his fingers. I can't wait for you to feel how good it is when we both take you."

Shivering, she cried out, redoubling her efforts on my thick shaft. I closed my eyes at the overwhelming sensation as her small body quaked between us, writhing from the force of her orgasm.

My head fell back, the pleasure of watching her reach her joy too much for me. Spine aching from the pressure, I thrust into her mouth one last time, needing to spill down her throat. Seed burst forth, trickling from the corners of her mouth.

I eased away from her swollen lips, wiping her face with

the corner of the sheet as Justin pulled her into his arms. I laid down on her other side, breathing hard as I tried to regain my senses.

"Sleep," Justin murmured. "We'll have a short rest."

Her breath evened into sleep and we dozed with her, content to have our wife in our arms.

Justin poked me some time later, rousing me from my nap. "What?" I asked, scowling as I sat up.

"Where's Maddy?"

I glanced down at the space between us where our wife should have been sleeping, then laid a hand on the cold sheets. "She's been gone for awhile," I replied, lunging to my feet. "Get dressed."

We dashed into the kitchen, our hearts sinking with dismay when we found her coat and boots missing, along with her clothes.

"She might have gone to the barn," Justin said, pulling on his boots.

"I doubt she's gone far. We weren't asleep that long."

Unfortunately, she wasn't to be found. None of the saddles were missing, but that didn't mean much for Maddy. A quick scan of the surrounding area revealed nothing.

"She has to be here somewhere," Justin said, pointing at her horse. "She wouldn't have left us without him."

"Let's go find her."

———

MADDY

HOPING my husbands were still sleeping, I returned from the creek with the products of my labors, including fresh-caught trout and morel mushrooms for our supper. Mercy, they'd about knocked the good sense from my head with their antics, yet my insides still quivered with delight. I was most assuredly a wanton creature for wanting them so much.

As I opened the door, Caleb dashed across the pasture and grabbed my shoulders.

I jumped and let out a surprised gasp. "My goodness—"

"Where have you been?" he demanded.

Laying a hand on my chest in an attempt to calm my racing heart, I said, "Lord have mercy, Caleb. You frightened the life from me."

"You were frightened? We woke up and you were gone." Justin said, taking the fish from me. "Where did you get these?"

"The stream in the horse pasture. They're for supper. There's barely enough food for a week in your pantry."

My husbands stared at me as if I'd grown a second head. "You went...fishing?" Caleb asked.

"I found mushrooms and early greens too. I mean to feed you both a decent meal. Where did you two head off to?"

"We were looking for you," Justin replied, giving me a dark stare that faded into a reluctant smile. "But I think I'm more interested in what you're making for supper."

Caleb shot him a look, still frowning. "First things first," he said. "You're not to go haring off like that without telling us where you're going."

"I..." I blinked up at his stern face. "I'm sorry."

Without warning, I burst into tears and flung myself into Caleb's arms. Justin dropped the fish and hugged me from behind, trying to calm my crying with soft whispers in my ear.

"It's all right, sweetheart. We aren't mad," he crooned, petting my hair. "Why are you crying?"

"Did you get hurt?" Caleb asked.

Sniffing, I lifted my face from Caleb's chest and wiped my tears with the back of my hand. "No, it's just...nobody's worried about me like that in a long time. I'm sorry I took off. I didn't think anyone would care."

———

JUSTIN

I FELT LIKE A HEEL. Here I was, looking down at a mess of fine fish and yelling at our wife for doing what must come naturally to her. She was an independent, capable young woman, certainly not the pampered princess we'd expected. Looking at Caleb, I knew he was thinking the same thing.

"We do care," I said firmly, moving so she faced both of us, then leaning to kiss her forehead. "Your safety is important to us. Montana can be a dangerous place. No one goes off without telling someone."

"But we're sorry we yelled at you," Caleb added, also giving her a kiss. "We won't do it again if you promise to let one of us know where you're going."

Maddy gave us a shaky smile and nodded. "I promise."

She threw herself into our arms, and my heart swelled in my chest as I stroked her fiery hair. I wanted to take her right back to bed and show her how happy she made us, but she'd gone to so much trouble and effort to please us, I couldn't let her work go to waste. Stepping back, I picked up the fish.

"What do you plan to do with these fine trout, Miss Maddy?" I asked.

Dimples lit up her cheeks when she grinned. "After you and Caleb finish cleaning them, I'll roast them with some salt and herbs I found, plus the mushrooms."

"Mushrooms?" Caleb asked, glancing at her sharply. "You have to be careful with mushrooms."

"I know." She nodded, then frowned as she swatted at a mosquito as big as a hummingbird. "You have a fine patch of morels in the woods. They're easy to recognize. Can't believe you didn't know they were there."

We shrugged, then Caleb said, "I didn't know they were edible. Aside from that, neither of us can cook."

"Ah. Well, it would be a help if you'd clean those trout. I'll get the greens started and cook up some fried mush to go with it."

She sailed inside, leaving us to our task. My mouth watering for the promised supper, I sat on the stoop and grabbed a fish. "Get to work, or I'll eat your share," I muttered to Caleb.

"Fat chance." He sat next to me, retrieving his belt knife. Laughing softly, he shook his head. "How is it we're outside cleaning fish when we were supposed to be yelling at her?"

"She didn't do anything wrong," I corrected. "Besides, she caught 'em. It's only fair that we clean 'em."

When we finished, we took her catch inside, then sat at the table while she worked. She obviously knew what she was about in a kitchen and delicious odors soon filled the room as she chatted happily with us. My stomach growled out a demand when she set plates loaded with food in front of us. Small rounds of fried cornmeal mush redolent of salt pork filled a basket set in the center of the table.

"Justin, will you say the blessing?" she asked, seating herself.

I did, thanking the Lord privately for Maddy. Caleb was probably doing the same thing. Tonight, we would show her how much her thoughtfulness meant to us.

10

ALEB

MERCY, I'd never had a meal so fine. Even Justin's mama, widely known as the best cook in three counties, didn't hold a candle to our sweet wife. I wondered what she'd do with a stocked pantry, and the thought nearly made me swoon. There would be cakes and preserves, and maybe even some huckleberry pies. The minute we got our cattle sold, we'd buy everything she'd need.

When we finished eating, I carried our plates to the sink, mixing hot water from the stove with soap.

"Caleb!" she scolded, trying to shoulder me out of the way. "You don't need to do that!"

Justin plucked her off her feet, then set her down in a chair with a cup of coffee. "Sit, Maddy. We'll clean."

Her lower lip trembled and she blinked. If she cried again, I was going to do something unseemly. But she didn't. Instead, she gave us a glorious smile, and said, "Thank you."

"It's the least we can do after such a fine meal," I said. "But we meant what we told you before our wedding. You don't have to cook if you don't want to."

Justin growled and shot me a glare, making her laugh. "Don't worry. As I said, I enjoy cooking. I'll do better when I have the proper supplies, but I'm glad you enjoyed it."

We looked at each other and didn't argue. I was having a hard time imagining better, and neither of us were going to stop her if it truly made her happy.

It almost seemed too good to be true. We had a good-natured, sweet wife with right fine skills in the kitchen. It made me doubly determined to make sure she was so well-pleasured in bed she'd never have reason to regret our hasty marriage.

When we finished, we took her outside for a short walk as the sun set to let her explore our land. Although the evening was fine, she refused to leave without her coat. I nodded in tacit approval. She'd already learned her lesson about the vagaries of Montana weather, it seemed.

Our cattle ranged around us, gathered in tight knots as evening fell. Frowning, I did a quick head count. "Looks like we're missing a few," I murmured to Justin.

"Missing?" Maddy asked. "What do you mean, missing? How on earth do you lose a cow?"

"Rustlers, sometimes, but usually bears or wolves," I replied.

"Oh." She flushed and lowered her head. "Maybe I shouldn't go off by myself. Don't know why that didn't occur to me. Do you think it's animals?"

Laughing, Justin wrapped an arm around her shoulder. "We don't have too much trouble with critters. They usually stay away, but it's spring now, and they'll be out and about. Aside from that, we'd have found the leftovers."

"Rustlers then."

"No, probably not," I said. "We'd have heard word from other ranchers."

"Hmm. Suppose we ought to look for them," she murmured. "If it's not animals or rustlers, they've either wandered to someone else's land or they're still here."

"We've looked," Justin said. "Can't find hide nor hair of any of them."

"Let's get back home," I suggested. "It's getting late, and we've had a busy day."

"We slept for most of it," Maddy countered, her eyes sparkling.

"That means we have plenty of strength to make love to our wife." I swung her into my arms, making her giggle.

She squirmed, her curves enticing me. I'd have to find a chunk of hardwood and get started carving a plug for our pretty wife's bottom. I couldn't wait to get her trained to accept both of us. My shaft hardened and strained against my trousers at the thought. Lengthening my stride, I walked faster.

I set her down on the stoop and Justin nearly tore her dress getting it off her, leaving her bare. Her pale skin gleamed in the setting sun, making her look like a Titian painting.

"It's not dark yet!" she protested, covering herself with bare arms. The evening chill made gooseflesh rise on her body and we hustled her inside. I wanted to make love to her in a sun-drenched meadow under the wide Montana sky, but it would have to wait until summer.

We took her to bed, our exertions soon warming her until sweat glistened on her body. She might not be ready to take both of us, but there were other ways to give our wife the ultimate pleasure.

"On your knees," I ordered.

Her eyes glazed with passion, she obeyed, turning to look at me over her shoulder. Justin touched her cheek, making her look at him.

"Open, sweetheart." He brushed her lips with the crown of his member, pulling the foreskin back as he painted them with droplets of moisture leaking from the tip.

She let out a soft moan as her lips parted and her channel clenched around me when she took him into her mouth. I surged into her. Maddy sucked him deeply, letting him use her mouth with languid strokes as she whimpered around the thick shaft.

"Look at you," I murmured, running a hand down her back. "You suck his cock so beautifully. And I love how you clench on me with your sweet pussy while I fuck you."

I coated my thumb with her juices and eased it into her back passage, making her choke out a pleasured cry. Her inner walls rippled and it was all I could do to control the overwhelming urge to spill inside her.

"We'll take you here soon," I crooned. "We'll fill both your holes at the same time, and you'll experience unimaginable pleasure."

Maddy bucked, slamming her hips against me. In an effort to keep her still, I grabbed her hair, pulling gently on the long curls until she lifted her face. Justin took advantage of her new position and sank balls deep into her welcoming mouth, groaning in pleasure as his eyes fell shut.

Our wife seemed to like a bit of dominance in bed, and we were more than happy to give it to her. I let go of her hair and reached between her thighs for the bundle of nerves that would give her delight. When I touched it, just a bare brush of my fingers across her most sensitive place, she screamed, the sound muffled by Justin's cock, then spasmed hard, her fierce orgasm pulling the seed from my balls in an uncontrollable rush.

Justin shouted and thrust deeply, cutting off her cries as he emptied himself into her swollen mouth. Between us, she fell to the bed, exhausted and replete.

She hummed softly while we cleaned her, then drifted off as we spooned her between us.

———

MADDY

STRETCHING, I allowed myself the luxury of waking slowly, my body sore in all the right places. It was barely dawn and my husbands still slept next to me. Although I shivered with renewed need, there was work to be done, and I'd been lazy enough.

They'd turned me into a wanton, my two husbands, and I wasn't a bit sorry.

When I attempted to wriggle free, Justin caught me, pulling me back into his long arms. Huffing out a breath, I said, "I have to go make breakfast."

Caleb pulled Justin's arms off me, then rolled me out of bed, neat as you please. When Justin grumbled, he said, "We don't get in Maddy's way when she has cooking on her mind."

Justin cracked an eye open, then sat up. "No idea what I was thinking." He grinned at me, his dark brown eyes crinkled with humor. "I'd be a fool to stop you. What's for breakfast?"

"Normally, I'd say a mess of eggs and flapjacks, along with bacon or ham, but it's going to be leftovers from last night." I opened the satchel Ann had given me, searching for a clean dress. "Sure you don't want to ride into town for supplies?"

"Temptress," Caleb muttered tossing a pillow at me.

I laughed and tossed it back, accidentally on purpose hitting him in the face. Sobering, I said, "We can't live on beans and a little flour forever, and you know it. At the very least, one of us needs to hunt up a deer or cull one of your cows."

They grumbled and didn't look at me. My husbands might not want to admit I was right, but I was willing to let it go for now. If they continued to be stubborn, I'd make my way into town myself. When I reached into the satchel once more, my hand closed on a small wooden box. I pulled it out and opened it, revealing a strange bulb-shaped wooden object with a narrow end and a wide base, along with a small glass bottle.

"What's this?" I asked, holding it up. "Looks like some fancy decoration for something."

An evil gleam lit in Justin's eyes and Caleb laughed outright, taking it from me. "Oh, honey, it is a decoration and just the thing we needed."

"What's it for?" I reached for it again, but he wouldn't give it back. "It looks like the top of a bedpost, excepting for that wide base at the bottom."

Still grinning, he wiped the object with a cloth and water from the pitcher, then opened the glass bottle and coated the wood with glistening moisture.

Justin put his hands on my shoulders, then gently pushed down until I was bent over, my elbows resting on the bed. "What are you doing? I thought I was going to cook breakfast."

I felt very exposed with my bottom in the air. The

position reminded me of Celeste and her cane, but Caleb's warm hand on my hip comforted me. He and Justin had been so angry when they saw the scars she'd left, and I was sure they weren't about to hurt me.

"This is a toy used to train Mohamiran wives for their husbands," Caleb replied. "It will go in your bottom to make you ready for us."

The rounded tip of the toy touched my bottom and I clenched down. It was dirty! That was not a place where things should go in. Justin kissed my shoulders, letting his lips glide over my chilled flesh.

"Shh, sweetheart. It won't hurt, and I promise you'll like it," he murmured against my ear.

I relaxed, soothed by his words as Caleb worked the plug inside me. Justin was right. Aside from a slight stretching sensation, it didn't hurt at all. They helped me straighten and I gasped as it shifted inside me, sparking nerves to life.

Turning me to face the door, Justin swatted my bottom, then said, "You were going to make breakfast, correct?"

"But...I'm not dressed!"

"All the better to keep you inside," Caleb replied, crossing his arms over his wide chest. "If we keep you naked, you won't be tempted to run off."

"Oh! But what if someone comes?" I shivered and reached for the satchel. I felt...strange. The plug moved with me, making my woman's flesh clench around nothing. How did they expect me to be able to think with this tease of pleasure dancing just out of my reach?

I drew my hand back, giving up my protests. This was what they wanted of me, and I'd promised to obey. Besides, I was sure they wouldn't let anyone see me like this.

Bare as the day I was born, I reheated breakfast, thankful they allowed me an apron for the chore. When everything was ready, they took it away again. Seated on Justin's lap, they fed me, teasing me with glancing touches that never went where I needed them most. By the time we finished eating, I was a panting mess and there was a wet spot on Justin's trousers.

Although I expected them to give up our tantalizing games, they didn't. After three days suffering their temptation, I was ready to burst! Although they always satisfied me in bed after sundown, my days were spent naked with a plug in my bottom, and I was never left alone. While one worked, the other would tease me to distraction, fucking me with that infernal plug.

They had me so muddled and turned around, I'd barely thought about Prince in days, or how I planned to feed three people with dwindling supplies. I decided to put my foot down and make them cease their maddeningly provocative behavior.

Unfortunately, the thought scurried away like a startled chipmunk when Caleb crooked a finger and pointed at the floor between his splayed knees. I knelt before him, addled and addicted to his taste and touch, just as I was for Justin's.

———

JUSTIN

I STROKED the tangled mess of red hair away from Maddy's face, smiling fondly. We'd driven her to distraction for several days, finally quieting her protests of needing to work. She didn't have to though. We wanted her to have a life of ease and comfort.

Unfortunately, that wasn't Maddy's way, and despite her sensual bliss, she grew restless.

"We have to let her go," Caleb murmured, his voice barely audible.

I stiffened and bristled, then realized he meant we had to release her from our games and let her work. Aside from that, whoever wasn't with Maddy was doing the labor of two men. We wouldn't be able to keep up much longer, and we did need her help.

The list of things she was capable of, spat at us like bullets over supper the night we claimed her as ours, itched at both of us. As much as we wanted her safe and comfortable, she wouldn't be happy, and she'd been right. We needed her. Smiling down at her wistfully, I acknowledged the thought that we needed her more than she needed us. She made us a family.

Leaning close, I kissed her, inhaling her sweet perfume. "Ready to wake up, darling?"

"A few more minutes," she muttered, burying her face in my chest.

"We thought you might like to see Prince," Caleb said. "I'm sure he misses you."

"Dressed?" She cracked an eye open and glared at us.

"Yes, and you should pick a saddle from the barn."

Sitting up, she stretched, revealing the knobs of her spine. "No plug today?"

"No. Not today. We thought you might like to ride out."

Leaping from the bed, Maddy rummaged in her satchel for a clean dress and pulled it over her head. Scant seconds later, she was in the kitchen and reheating beans for our breakfast. She shoveled food into her mouth, clearly in a hurry to get outside. Her impatience was obvious when we lingered over our meal. I had no idea what she did to plain beans to make them taste so good.

"Go," Caleb finally said. "We'll clean..."

The door slammed behind her, making me chuckle as I sipped my coffee.

"...up." He shook his head and grinned at me. "And, she's gone," he said, still smiling.

I finished my coffee and stood. "Means we'd best get on with our chores too."

We spent the day repairing fences and scowling at our dwindling herds. Where were they all going? Every steer was money we couldn't use to support our beautiful new wife, and I wasn't having it. I raked my hands through the stubble on my head, reminding myself to have Caleb or Maddy take care of the chore later.

"Where are they?" I finally burst out. We should have at least fifty new calves, but there were barely twenty, and no sign of intruders, either animal or man.

"I have no idea." Caleb chewed his lower lip, then smiled wryly when his attention caught on our wife riding her stallion bareback through our southernmost pasture where our cows should be. Her hair flowed behind her as she sat a neat canter, her small booted feet steady on his sides. She must not have found a saddle that suited her, and had a rope tied to Prince's halter in place of reins.

"Good afternoon, gentlemen," she said. "Does your brand look like this?"

When she drew the shape in the air with one graceful hand, I nodded. "Why do you ask?"

"I found about eighty head at the base of the escarpment. There's a trail leading down behind a pine thicket. I wouldn't have seen it at all, excepting for the heifer that made her way through while I watched."

"Show us," Caleb ordered.

"No."

We blinked at her as she sat her horse primly, her chin set with determination. We'd promised ourselves Maddy would never know physical punishment from us, but I was an inch away from taking off my belt.

My jaw tightened painfully, but I made an effort to speak calmly. "Why not, Maddy?"

"I want to go to town tomorrow."

"No. Not by yourself, and we don't have time to—"

"Justin, we're out of beans," she snapped. "There's enough left for tomorrow, but we'll all be going hungry after that. I told you three days ago."

"Can't you just gather food like you did before?"

Sighing, she pinched the bridge of her nose. "Yes, but it takes time, and doesn't help with everything else that needs doing. Aside from that, I want eggs and roast chicken. I want sugar, and I want to put in a vegetable garden so I have something to preserve for winter. I want hogs for bacon and ham, and a case of good bourbon." She leaned over Prince's withers, pinning us with her glare. "You told me I could use my savings for things I wanted. That is what I want."

Caleb and I exchanged a glance, then nodded reluctantly.

11

ALEB

As much as I wanted to, I couldn't argue with her. An extra mouth meant our food stores hadn't lasted as long and there had been little enough to begin with. Even if she hadn't backed us into a corner with her bargain, we would have needed to make a trip sooner than I'd planned. Her description of what she wanted made me drool in anticipation of what she'd make with all those things.

Squealing happily, Maddy led us to the trail she found and started down, laying almost prone on Prince's rump as he negotiated the steep path. We followed her and I blinked. We'd always thought this section of our property was inaccessible. Although it had ample grazing and a water source, we hadn't managed to find a good route around the sheer cliff. Dozens of new calves capered around their mothers, strong and healthy. All the cattle we were missing appeared to be here, plus a few from my neighbors.

"How are we going to get them back up?" Justin asked.

"No idea."

Maddy chewed on her lower lip, looking worried. "Drive them up a few at a time? Maybe lure them with salt? I don't know what cows want, but there has to be another way down."

"Let's try the salt," I finally said. "There are a few blocks in the barn."

"Once we get them up, we're going to build a fence here," Justin muttered, his face set in a scowl. He wasn't any happier about the situation than I was, but at least we'd found our missing stock, thanks to Maddy. If she did nothing else, she ensured we'd keep our livelihood. My thoughts turned to the reward Caleb and I would give her after supper, and my shaft hardened.

"A strong one," Maddy muttered, making us laugh. She scowled at us, then said, "I'm going fishing before I decide they'll make fine roast beef."

We let her go to town the next morning, her stallion hitched to our old buckboard wagon, with stern instructions to be home before sunset. Even though Bridgewater was safe and she'd be looked after, we worried. Of course, she'd made her way from Kentucky by herself. I imagined a five-mile trip into town posed no great challenge for such a woman.

To our surprise, most of our missing stock were where they belonged, lured by the salt. The few remaining head wandered up without being driven and Justin went to their owners to make arrangements for their return.

When he returned from his errand, we started on the endless list of chores, both of us casting glances at the lane as we waited for Maddy to come home. As an afterthought, I remembered to sweep out the pantry and ready it for

Maddy's purchases. Although we hadn't wanted to let her go, Justin and I both looked forward to something besides beans.

She'd been gone less than eight hours, and my cock was already bursting. Barely a day went by that one or both of us didn't make love to her after lunch, and it was almost sundown.

We finished our work and I scowled at the lowering sun. We were both exhausted and hungry, but that wouldn't stop us from giving Maddy a stern talking-to when she deigned to show up. As if summoned by my thought, a cloud of dust rose in the distance, resolving itself into the form of our wife driving a heavily laden wagon.

Lathered and tired, Prince's head drooped as she stopped him in front of the cottage. We unharnessed him quickly, and Justin led him to the barn for a well-deserved rubdown.

"Sorry I'm late," she murmured, leaning into my arms. "It took a while to get everything loaded." Turning to the wagon, she lifted out a box and smiled when she peered inside. "Say hello to your future eggs. Your bourbon-cured bacon is still in the wagon."

The box contained dozens of fluffy yellow chicks. I laughed and took it from her, then set it in the kitchen next to the stove. Pouring her a cup of coffee, I pointed at a kitchen chair. "Sit and rest. I'll unload the wagon."

She didn't argue, meaning she was more tired than she was willing to admit. There were sacks of flour, cornmeal, and sugar, along with small barrels of salt pork and lard. Aside from that, six weanling hogs squealed in wooden cages. An obviously pregnant heifer chewed her cud behind the wagon, still tethered. Apparently, Maddy wanted fresh milk too.

Justin returned from caring for her horse, and raised an eyebrow at the hogs. "We have an extra stall in the barn. Suppose we'll just put them in there until we can build a pen."

"She's got chickens too. They're in a box next to the stove in the kitchen."

His eyes lit on the heifer and he smiled. "And butter. We'll have butter soon."

Lord have mercy, we hadn't had butter in an age.

After a few weeks, it was almost as if Maddy had been part of our lives forever. We spent every night loving her into sated bliss, but we still hadn't taken that last step of making her truly ours.

It wasn't for lack of want, but rather for lack of time. Spring on a cattle ranch was busy. Her chickens were growing and safely in their coop. The hogs were fat and sassy, and we had plenty of milk and butter. The delights from Maddy's kitchen made Justin and I nearly swoon with joy.

The night before the annual community cattle drive to the railhead in Butte, she even made fried hand pies with a sack of dried apples she'd hidden from us. The minute I tasted the crisp, flaky pastry, I about died and went to heaven. We used her beautiful body as our plate, eating the sweet treat from her quivering belly with fluffy whipped cream.

———

AS WE PREPARED TO LEAVE, I touched the box containing the plug and the special oil we used to prepare it for her. When we got back from our trip, we'd have our wife to ourselves and there would be more than enough time and leisure to claim her in the way of Mohamiran husbands.

Justin and I looked forward to buying her all the luxuries she'd been denied. Cigars and bourbon, plus new dresses and underthings made of silk. She never once complained, but we wanted those things for her.

"You ready?" Justin asked, chewing on a flaky biscuit.

I buttoned my trousers and nodded, then swallowed the last of my coffee and walked into the kitchen.

Her smile sweet and wistful, Maddy handed me a biscuit, then reached up to kiss my cheek. "I'll miss you two."

I shared a glance with Justin, then swept her into my arms and carried her back to bed. The rest of the crew could wait. We had a duty to our wife.

———

MADDY

I WAVED as my husbands rode away, keeping a smile plastered to my face as the predawn sky swallowed them up. They'd be back by supper tomorrow, but we hadn't spent a night apart since our hasty wedding. I didn't look forward to sleeping in that big empty bed by myself.

It might be only one night, but I wouldn't see them for two full days. I shook my head and got started with my chores. There was plenty of work to keep me occupied. In the unlikely event I ran out of things to do, there were still several horses needing my attention.

When I finished, I glanced up at the sun. If I hurried, I had time to ride into town to see if Mr. Fuller had replied to my letter asking him to sell the property in Kentucky. I shook my head and got to work scrubbing the kitchen floor. It was too soon for a response from him. I would just have to be patient. Besides, I'd promised Caleb and Justin I wouldn't leave the ranch and I didn't want to disappoint them.

I wanted everything perfect for when Justin and Caleb got home. Nothing would interrupt our reunion night. My core twitched with need, and I redoubled my efforts on the floor. Staying busy would hopefully keep my mind off what I'd be missing.

Someone knocked, making me startle and bump my head on the edge of the stove. Rubbing the sore spot, I stood and walked to the door, wondering if Ann had come for a visit. The company would be nice.

Opening the door, I smiled, then blinked in surprise at two strange men. Another, wearing a silver star identifying him as a sheriff, stood behind them. My heart leapt in my chest and I staggered.

"Are Caleb and Justin all right?" I asked, grabbing for the doorframe.

"Mrs. Mathis, My name is Sheriff Baker. These two men have a warrant for your arrest. They're here to take you back to Kentucky," he said, his voice gentle. A fleeting expression of sympathy crossed his face before it smoothed into impassiveness.

"On what charge?"

"Horse theft." One of the men, a rotund fellow with cold gray eyes perused me, looking me up and down like a side of meat. "You've been accused of stealing a valuable stallion from Nathan Bergman."

"He has nothing I want," I retorted. "And he wouldn't know a valuable horse if it bit him in his skinny backside."

Sheriff Baker snorted, ignoring the taller man's look of disgust.

Grabbing my arm, the short man pulled me from the house, leaving the door stand open. "The warrant says otherwise. Do you still have the horse?"

"What horse? I didn't steal a thing from that awful man."

The second man, a tall specimen with bulging muscles, backhanded me, making me fall to the ground. "A palomino stallion," he snapped. "Where is he?"

I spat at his feet, then rubbed blood away from my cut lip. "I don't have him," I lied.

"If you hit her again while you're in my jurisdiction, I'll have you in jail so fast your heads will spin," the sheriff warned, gently helping me to my feet. "In fact, if I find out you've abused her at all, you'll be hearing from me." Giving the two bounty hunters a disgusted look, he added, "Do you see a palomino stallion?"

They glanced around, then shrugged. "It doesn't matter," the tall one snapped. "The bounty is only for her. Someone else can come catch the horse."

The short one slapped manacles on my wrists and ankles, then marched me to a wagon. Picking me up, the tall one dumped me in the back, attaching a piece of chain to my wrists.

I got to my knees, meeting the sheriff's eyes. "Tell my husbands what happened," I ordered. "And find someone to feed my animals while I'm gone."

He nodded as the wagon jerked into motion, knocking me off balance. I fell heavily, hitting my temple against the wood planks making up the bed. My head spun and I gritted my teeth against the pain, then huddled in a ball as best I could.

Less than an hour later, I was on a train headed back to the place I swore I'd never see again.

"I hear tell the women here take two men," the short man said, giving me a speculative look as he licked his lips.

"Disgusting." The tall one spat, looking directly at me. "Suffer not a whore to live. Too bad they won't hang her for horse theft."

"You got the bible quote wrong," I retorted. "Your intellect leaves something to be desired. Aside from that, I'm a married woman."

His fists clenched, but there were too many people in the car giving him sour glares for him to risk striking me again. Still, I wasn't going to press my luck any further.

Justin and Caleb would come for me. I crossed my fingers and toes, uncaring if the bounty hunters saw, then sent a prayer to the Lord.

———

JUSTIN

OUR HORSES WERE TIRED, but we hurried home as best we could. Maddy would have our hides if we pushed them too hard. Aside from that, they'd been good mounts for us during the cattle drive to the railhead, thanks to her schooling them.

I grinned at Caleb, tapping the pocket containing our accounting from the cattle broker. We'd be paid when they reached the stockyards in Laredo, and it was more than enough to keep us comfortably for another year.

Returning my smile, he said, "Ready to see our wife?"

"Bath first, then wife. We're not going to her bed until we don't stink."

"Wonder if she'll have supper waiting."

I laughed outright, startling the horses a bit. "You know she will. She'll be expecting us. I'm more looking for a bath and taking her straight to bed."

We rode up to the house, and my heart fell when Maddy didn't rush out to meet us. From the coop, her chickens squalled angrily, and the hogs set up a racket too.

Caleb frowned, dismounting. "I'll see to the pigs."

Once we got the animals cared for, we went inside, finding the house empty. "Where is she?" I asked. "Think we ought to check the trout stream?"

"Something's wrong. I don't think she's on the ranch."

"Do you think she took off?" I shook my head in denial. Our Maddy wouldn't do that, but her boots were gone.

"Prince is still in the pasture," he said, heading into our bedroom.

I let out a sigh of relief. She wouldn't have left without her horse. When he returned, I scowled at the object in his hands. It was the cloth purse holding Maddy's nest egg. He opened it and gasped, then emptied it to the table. A roll of banknotes as big around as my fist tumbled out.

"She wouldn't have left without this either," he murmured.

"Let's check the creek. Maybe she didn't see us ride up." Caleb nodded and followed me out.

As we left the house, a rider tore down our lane, his horse lathered and blowing hard. When he got closer, I recognized him and lifted a hand in greeting. "Sheriff Baker," I called. "What brings you out this way?"

Caleb frowned, but shook the sheriff's hand politely after he dismounted.

"Two bounty hunters came for your Maddy yesterday," he said, his voice gruff. "They had a warrant for her arrest on charges of horse theft and an extradition order."

"Damnation! You know she's no thief."

Caleb's face twisted and darkened. "What the hell were you thinking, letting them take our wife?"

Looking suddenly tired, Sheriff Baker shook his head. "I didn't have a choice. The warrant was legitimate. I sent the telegram checking it out myself."

My knees buckled and I wished I had something to hang on to. "We'll follow and get her back."

"You can catch the early train tomorrow and be only a few days behind her," Sheriff Baker replied. "You should also bring your marriage certificate, and any other documentation you can find. Andrew and Robert told me the fellow who's accusing her wanted her for his wife. If she's already married, he might give up this fool plan."

When we nodded, he mounted his tired horse. "Best of luck to you both. We'll be keeping you and Maddy in our prayers."

He rode away and we went inside, staring down at the money laying on the table. I untied the string holding the bundle together and blinked.

"There has to be over five hundred dollars," I breathed.

Caleb grunted. "I feel like an idiot. She had all this money sitting here, and I was complaining about buying food."

"That's a whole lot of stud fees, but at ten dollars a head, I can see it. Wonder how much she had to start."

"Doesn't matter." Caleb took the money from me and replaced it. "It's hers, and she'll tell us if she wants to."

"The bank won't open until after the morning train leaves. We have to use some of it for—"

"No. We promised she could keep her savings for things she wanted. Not for us."

I arched a brow. This wouldn't be a problem if we'd already been paid for our cows. "I'm thinking Maddy would want us to get her out of this mess. Don't you?"

A few lines of tension faded from his face and he nodded. "You have the right of it," he finally said. "We'll replace it once we have her back."

"Let's get packed. We have a long road ahead of us."

12

ALEB

AFTER A SLEEPLESS NIGHT, we rode out to meet the train, leaving our horses with Andrew and Robert. Ann wrung her hands, tears sparkling in her blue eyes.

They weren't the only ones to see us off. All of Bridgewater came to pay their respects. Emma, wife to Whitmore Kane and Ian Monroe, brought us a large basket filled with food for the trip. Connor MacDonald and Dashiell McPherson's wife Rebecca gave us another. Several families pressed money on us, refusing to take no for an answer.

Ian shook his head and pressed a twenty-dollar bill into my hand. "Accept it. You may need it for her defense."

Andrew handed me an envelope as well. "There's enough for you to catch the express in Omaha. You'll get there faster."

"Right," Robert added. "We'll take care of your place until you bring her home."

There was nothing for it but to accept their generosity. Emotion clogged my throat and I nodded. Justin managed to thank everyone before we boarded the train. He'd always been the better of us at finding the right words to say.

Andrew had been right about the express in Omaha. We arrived before Maddy and got a room at a boardinghouse.

"I want to see this fellow Nathan," Justin muttered.

"Maddy said he's the saloon keeper," I replied, pointing at a two-story building across the street from the hotel. We went inside and bellied up to the bar. Giving us a quiet greeting, a barmaid wearing a dress that barely covered her brought us each a beer.

A lady sauntered inside, her straw hat perched at a jaunty angle on blonde curls. She sat at a table close behind us and tapped her parasol on the floor, wrinkling her nose at the barmaid. "Get me Nathan," she snapped.

"Yes, Miss Celeste." The barmaid scurried off and I allowed my lips to curl into a smirk.

"So, that's Maddy's stepmother," Justin whispered. "I wouldn't mind having a few words with her."

A lanky man with dark hair and a thin goatee joined her, kissing her cheek before sitting across the small table. "To what do I owe the honor of your presence, darling?"

"Madelaine will be here tomorrow," she replied in a low voice. "But there's a problem. The bounty hunters we sent say she's already married. I just got the telegram."

"So?"

"Nathan, don't you understand?" Celeste wrung her hands. "If the brat is married, it spoils all our plans. And once Fred Fuller hears about it, he won't represent you in court. You know how he dotes on her."

"Don't matter. She stole that horse." Nathan's face darkened and his lips twisted into an ugly sneer. "If she's in prison, her daddy's property reverts to you anyway. It'll serve the little bitch right for crossing us."

"What then? And what about this supposed husband?"

"We'll worry about it if he shows up. I made sure my men took her after he was gone on a cattle drive. It might be weeks before he finds out she's gone. You and I will marry, sell the place off, and split the money like we planned. Afterwards, we'll get an annulment." He patted her cheek, then added, "The best part is we're saved the trouble of getting rid of Maddy."

Celeste nodded and smiled. "Perfect. I'd been wondering what to do with her."

"She was going to have an unfortunate tumble down the stairs." He laid a hand over his heart. "Poor girl, in the prime of her life too."

I'd heard enough. "Let's go," I hissed softly to Justin. "We're done here."

Justin straightened as we walked out. "We need to see Fred Fuller," he said, his face rigid with fury.

I didn't blame him. I was fair itching to go back and rearrange Nathan's face. As much as the thought of hurting a woman disgusted me, I'd make an exception for Celeste.

We asked a boy for directions and twenty minutes later, we were having a very interesting conversation with Mr. Fuller. He was understandably livid.

Desperate for a way to exonerate Maddy, we poured over her father's will, knowing we were running out of time.

His brow knitted in concentration, Justin scanned a page we'd already looked at many times. My mama taught us both to read at the same time, but he'd always been better at it. Drawing a finger under one passage, he looked up. "Didn't Maddy say Prince was a gift?"

"Yes, her sixteenth birthday," I replied. "Why?"

"Says here all gifts to Maddy are hers and not part of the estate as long as—"

"They were given to her before she turned eighteen!" Mr. Fuller exclaimed, glee filling his voice. "How did I miss that?"

"The damned will is almost twenty pages," I muttered, glaring at the scattering of paper across the desk. I plucked up our marriage certificate and pocketed it, unwilling to let it out of my sight.

"Yes, but I wrote it," he replied, grinning at me. "That also means you're the legal owner of a thousand acres of prime land, Mr. Mathis. Maddy sent me a letter asking me to sell it, which was how we knew where to find her."

I blinked, then turned my gaze on Justin.

"Why didn't she tell us?" he asked.

Justin and I stared at each other, and I gave him a wry smile. "I expect she wanted to make sure we...I wasn't like Nathan Bergman," I replied, my heart swelling along with my cock. "She decided she wanted to stay in Montana, and knew we'd probably argue with her about selling her family home."

"That sounds like Maddy. Unfortunately, Nathan and Celeste caught wind of it and had the judge issue that warrant," Mr. Fuller replied, putting the will back in order.

"Which we know now is false," Justin said.

Looking at him with respect, Mr. Fuller said, "Mr. Mathis is lucky to have you. We wouldn't have caught it if not for your sharp eyes. You must be an excellent partner to have."

"Thank you kindly, sir," Justin replied, keeping to the story we'd given the older man. As much as he appeared to care for Maddy, there was no sense sharing our unique family situation with him.

We returned to the boardinghouse, grabbing a quick meal of fried chicken, cornbread, and boiled greens from the communal kitchen. It was good, but I was sure our wife could do better.

Tomorrow we would have her back between us where she belonged. We'd never let her out of our sight again.

———

MADDY

THE STREETS WERE quiet as my captors marched me across town to the tiny jail. I had a black eye, and my face was bruised and swollen, courtesy of the tall bounty hunter with a mean right hook and a sense of righteousness that turned violent at the least provocation.

Sheriff Jameson, whom I'd known since I was a little girl, met us at the door and scowled at the bruises. "You won't be paid the full bounty," he snapped. "It specifically said she was to be returned unharmed."

"It's not our fault she's clumsy," the small one said, smirking at me. "She fell a lot."

Sheriff Jameson's gaze softened. "Maddy, honey? Did they hit you?"

"Yes," I said, pointing at the tall one. "He did upon three occasions. I think one of my teeth is loose."

The next thing I knew, deputies swarmed the pair and arrested them. I tried to smile, but it hurt too much.

"Don't worry," Sheriff Jameson said, helping me to a chair. "I promise they won't be anywhere near you. I'll have the missus bring you clean clothes and a meal before court."

"May I wash?"

"Sure, sweetheart. We'll get some water heated for you." He smiled and patted my shoulder, then used a skeleton key to release the shackles around my wrists and ankles.

I tried not to flinch, but the gentle touch hurt. My whole body ached. Between the beatings and being forced to sit still for hours on end during the interminable train trip, I was lucky I could move at all.

Mrs. Jameson bustled in, followed by Dahlia. Letting out a soft cry of distress, Dahlia rushed to me and pulled me into a hug. Tears streamed from her eyes as she pulled away, still holding my arms.

"I'm so sorry," she whispered. "I tried to tell everyone you were married, but nobody cared. I wish I'd never—"

"It's all right," I said firmly. "My husband will come for me." I almost said husbands, but cut the word off just in time.

Unfortunately, my arrest was valid. I had stolen Prince. I didn't know if I would do things differently though. I shook the thought away. I'd already made my choices and I'd have to live with the consequences. At the very least, Celeste would get thrown out on her ear when Caleb came. I smiled at the thought. I might not have much, but I'd get to imagine my nasty stepmother being homeless. Best of all, Nathan would end up with nothing.

Dahlia and Mrs. Jameson hustled me into a cell and covered the bars with a blanket to protect my modesty. Unfortunately, sound carried and when they cried out in dismay at the scattering of bruises on my body, Sheriff Jameson came running. His feet stalled and he let out a vicious curse before turning the other way.

Lifting my chin, I let them bathe the filth from my body. It felt good to be clean again and I didn't protest when they slid a slightly worn calico dress over my head. Thankfully, they didn't insist on a corset. I was too sore for that.

After finishing a delicious breakfast of bacon and eggs with biscuits and peppered gravy, it was time to go to the courthouse for my trial. I thought I wouldn't be able to eat, but I had faith. Caleb and Justin would come for me. I just knew they would. Sheriff Baker from Bridgewater would have wasted no time in telling them, and they had plenty of money in my nest egg.

I chewed my lip as we approached the courthouse and crossed my fingers. They'd have train fare if Caleb thought to look. The man was too stubborn by half.

Sheriff Jameson ushered me toward the courtroom, a gentle hand on my elbow. He'd been overly solicitous of me, and very careful not to touch my injuries. He was a good man and I didn't fault him for doing his job.

When the door opened, my feet went numb and I stilled. Caleb and Justin were sitting with Mr. Fuller, smiling at me. Oh, how I wanted to run to them! Missing them was a physical ache, and now that it was gone, I couldn't wait to pull them into my arms and let them take me to bed. Unfortunately, Sheriff Jameson's hand on my elbow reminded me where I was.

Mr. Fuller stood and went into the antechamber behind the bench, his hands filled with papers. Urging me forward, the sheriff helped me to sit between my husbands, then strode to the back of the courtroom near the door.

Nathan sat on the other side, his face set in a nasty smirk. I shuddered and resolved to ignore him. A quick glance over my shoulder revealed Celeste, trying to hide under one of her ridiculous hats.

"Lord have mercy, sweetheart, you're a sight for sore eyes," Justin whispered, careful of his words and the distance between us. "But you need to tell us who did that to your pretty face."

"The bounty hunters," I whispered back. "But they're in jail already."

"Good." Caleb took my hand and brought it to his lips. I wished I could kiss him and Justin both, but it was neither the time nor the place. "We'll get everything taken care of."

"How?" I lowered my head and tried to keep the tears at bay. "I did steal Prince."

"Wait and see," Justin whispered mysteriously.

"Order in the court! All rise for the honorable Judge Wentworth Gilbert."

We sat when the judge nodded. After a moment, he said, "There's some irregularity in this trial, so I'm going to sum up what I've just been told."

"Your honor, I object!" Nathan shouted. "This is—"

"This is my courtroom," Judge Gilbert announced. "Sit down, Mr. Bergman."

I shifted uncomfortably in my chair and glanced at my husbands for support. Both wore pleased smiles, but that made no sense. As far as I could tell, there wasn't anything to smile about. I wanted to ask what they planned, yet I couldn't risk annoying Judge Gilbert.

Judge Gilbert looked up at me and frowned. "Baby girl, what happened to your face?"

"The bounty hunters Mr. Bergman sent after her, your honor," Sheriff Jameson called from the back. "I already have them in custody."

"Good. I'll deal with them later." He shuffled paper into a stack, then looked up. "Mr. Fuller has produced documentation regarding Madelaine O'Connor Mathis. She is indeed married to the gentleman sitting next to her." Giving me a smile, he nodded. "I also have her late father's will before me."

Nathan slammed his fist on the table in front of him. "Why are we discussing this? Madelaine stole that horse from me."

"Be silent before I hold you in contempt!"

Leaning back in his chair, Nathan stewed, shooting me a virulent glare. I shivered at the hate in his eyes.

"As I was saying, on page nine, paragraph six, subsection two, the late Dr. O'Connor's will stipulates all gifts given to Maddy before her eighteenth birthday belong to her in their entirety. Since I know perfectly well her stallion sired two of my best horses before then, there is no question Prince's ownership is solely hers."

Nathan's face turned red with fury and he stood, pounding on the table once more. "Your honor—"

"Mr. Bergman, do not push me. You are a single word away from a contempt charge, and you'll be lucky if Maddy's husband doesn't have you charged with false imprisonment. Prince was sold to you illegally. If you want your money back, take it up with the woman who sold what didn't belong to her."

"I have the receipt for his purchase, along with his pedigree," I said, shooting a satisfied glare at Nathan. I wished I'd read that will closer, but I'd been so despondent over losing Daddy, I hadn't had the heart for it. Then again, if I'd read it, I'd have told Celeste and Nathan to go hang and wouldn't have met my husbands.

Ann's words about being glad she hadn't escaped made a lot more sense now.

My thoughts drifted to what would happen with Caleb and Justin after Judge Gilbert finished with us. Shaking my head, I tried to focus and dispel the sudden surge of heat lighting up my cheeks. I ached for their touch and my pussy grew wet and clenched with desire.

"That won't be necessary." The judge smiled at me, then turned his gaze on Caleb. "Now, if I was a proper husband to our sweet girl, I'd be thinking of ways to make the blackguard across the courtroom sorry for his actions. I recommend against it unless you're sure you won't get caught."

"Thank you for the advice, your honor."

"No charge. As I was saying, we have another issue regarding this will. Now that Miss Maddy is rightfully married, ownership of the late Dr. O'Connor's property is yours and Maddy's held jointly in its entirety."

My breath caught and I looked down at my hands. That was it. My secret was out. I didn't want to see the expression on my husbands' faces and hunched my shoulders against what was sure to come. To my shock, Justin took my hand, hiding the motion under the table. "It's all going to be fine, love. We'll be fine."

His whispered words calmed my racing heart, but I didn't dare look at Caleb.

"Thank you, your honor. We'll decide what to do with the property in due time."

"Would that include bringing Maddy back to us?"

"If that's what she wants, yes sir," Caleb replied, his voice calm and soothing.

"Fair enough." He banged his gavel, then said, "This session is adjourned. All charges against Madelaine Mathis are dropped."

 USTIN

I RESISTED the urge to pull Maddy into my arms and kiss her soundly. Caleb couldn't do it either, not with so many people around. It didn't stop him from brushing his lips over her forehead.

Lord have mercy, I wanted to tie Nathan Bergman into a knot and beat him with a stick for what he'd tried. Knowing he'd get off scot free didn't sit well, but there wasn't much we could do. We had no evidence, aside from an overheard conversation.

"Your honor," Caleb said. "I would like the sheriff's assistance in getting Maddy's stepmother evicted from my property."

"Granted."

"No! That's my home!" Celeste cried.

Caleb left me with Maddy and sauntered toward her, his

blue eyes like chips of ice. "Really?" he asked in a silky voice. "Let's see if I remember this correctly. You were talking with Mr. Bergman over there in the saloon, and—"

"Shut your mouth," she hissed, panic filling her suddenly pallid face.

"As you say," he agreed, his expression hard. "I suggest you pack your things. I want you out before sunset."

We took Maddy home. Not to a tiny cottage in Montana, but to a palatial estate house on a hill surrounded by rich meadows and farmland. Whitewashed split rail fence surrounded divided pastures containing fat cattle and sleek horseflesh.

I pictured our wife sitting in one of the bentwood rockers on the expansive porch, a cigar in one hand and a glass of bourbon in the other. The house was grand, and I wouldn't blame her if she wanted to stay.

"Maddy, we can build you a veranda—"

"Maybe next summer." She walked into the house like a queen and went to the kitchen. Opening a cupboard, she retrieved a brown bottle. Instead of bothering with a glass, she tipped it up and pulled several swallows, then handed it to me. "Go on," she urged. "Aside from that bourbon, Kentucky can go hang itself."

The liquor flowed like heated silk down my throat. I grinned and handed it to Caleb. "Does that mean you're coming home?"

"It depends." She turned to face the window looking out over a pasture.

"On what?" Caleb asked, kissing her neck.

"Will you have me?" She turned to face us, her pretty face solemn. "I lied to both of you."

"Yes, I suppose you did." I gave her the bottle, then

kissed her, tracing her lower lip with my tongue. "Were you going to tell us about your father's bequest?"

"I was," she said firmly. "But then..." Her voice trailed off and she looked down.

"Then?" Caleb prompted.

"I was so happy, and I didn't...I was afraid you'd want to live here, and I didn't want to. I wanted to stay in Montana."

"Then that's what you'll have," I murmured. "We'll sell this place and take you home where you belong."

Caleb and I shared a glance. We wouldn't ever tell Maddy what we'd overheard in the saloon. She didn't need to know, and it would hurt her.

A door slammed, making Caleb scowl. "But first we have to get rid of the squatter," he grumbled in irritation.

"Sit," I urged Maddy. "We'll deal with Celeste."

"No. I need to do this." She straightened her spine and her chin went up. I'd never been prouder of a person in my life. All the blood in my body rushed to my hardening shaft, reminding me we'd have our wife in our bed tonight.

She strode into the entryway, her face set with determination as she faced down her nemesis. "Get your clothes and personal belongings, Celeste. I want you out of my house."

"How dare you?" Celeste puffed out her chest and strode across the room, then lifted her parasol. Her intent was clear, but we wouldn't allow her to strike our wife.

I snatched it away and handed it to Caleb before she could blink.

"You little..." Her eyes narrowed, then she stroked Caleb's arm. "You know," she purred, "I'll wager you could use a real woman in your life."

"I've already found one. Sadly, you don't fit the description."

"Enough." Maddy strode between them, her face set. "Get your hands off my husband."

Caleb pushed Maddy behind him, ignoring her protests. "Justin, will you help these deputies gather Celeste's belongings? She's upsetting my wife."

"Of course, sir," I replied, keeping our ruse intact. "Mrs. Mathis, which one is her bedroom?"

Maddy showed me, and I wasted no time throwing Celeste's things into satchels and carpet bags. The deputies kept her from stealing everything else. Despite her vociferous protests, we escorted her out after her things were packed, slamming the door behind her.

Once we were alone, Maddy leaned against the wall and let out a tremendous sigh. "Lord have mercy, that woman makes me tired."

Silently, I handed her a glass of bourbon. She drained it and held it out for a refill, closing her eyes.

"What do I do now?" she asked, addressing her question to no one in particular.

"We're gonna sit on the veranda, share some bourbon and a cigar, and you're going to take your ease," Caleb replied, gently touching her bruised face.

I wanted to spend some time educating Nathan Bergman on the treatment of a lady, but Maddy needed us more than I needed to beat him to a pulp.

Maddy's eyes sparkled with humor mixed with wistful sadness. "And talk about Egypt?"

"And talk about Egypt." I stroked a finger across her jaw, then leaned down for a kiss.

––––––

CALEB

. . .

ALTHOUGH MADDY NEEDED to rest and heal from her injuries, she absolutely refused to let us sleep in another room. Truth be told, Justin and I weren't all that happy about the idea either, so we spent our nights squeezed together in Maddy's childhood bed. As much as we wanted to take her in our arms and make love to her, she was too banged up and sore.

There were also people roaming through the house, meaning Justin had to be up and out of her bed before dawn so we weren't caught. We couldn't complain too much though. Sara, Maddy's old family cook, was every bit as good in the kitchen as our wife was. Aside from that, Sara was better at making her rest than we were.

Three days after her trial, we watched Maddy knead bread and decided she was well enough for the trip home. Her strong, capable hands on the dough made me hard in an instant. I wanted her touch and I was done waiting.

"Sara, will you help Maddy pack up her things? It's time we...I took my wife home."

The older woman blinked, then nodded. "Of course, sir. Mr. Carter can help me."

Maddy's smile blossomed like a rose, and she squealed as she raced to me. Hugging me tightly, she said, "I can't wait."

She kissed me, her tongue flicking out to tease at my lower lip. I bit back a groan as Justin coughed and shifted in his chair.

"Naughty," I murmured into her ear.

"Not yet. Just wait until I get you home."

Later, I escorted her around town to let her say goodbye to folks, then rode home for lunch. As we returned our horses to their stalls, I asked, "Are you sorry you won't be coming back?"

"No. I'm going to miss my friends, especially Dahlia and Reggie, but we can write letters. I want to be with you and Justin. I want our big bed, and I want to wake up in your arms after a night of loving."

I hurried her into the tack room, slamming the door shut behind us, then pulled her against me and sank my hands into her silky hair. Lowering my head, I took her mouth in a gentle kiss. When she whimpered and clutched at my shoulders, I traced a finger across a hardening nipple, then unbuttoned her bodice, revealing her tender buds to my wandering hands and eyes. I bent to pull one into my mouth and lifted her skirts. My hand found slick wetness and I pushed a finger inside her tight heat.

When she cried out, I cupped her wet flesh, rubbing the heel of my hand against the center of her pleasure. Setting damp kisses to her elegant throat, I whispered, "You'll want to be a good girl and be quieter. That is, unless you want your stable hands to find you all wet and needy with your skirts around your hips and my hand between your thighs."

"Oh, Caleb!" Spasming, she clenched around my fingers and let out a soft moan as boots sounded on the board floor just outside the door. I recognized the sound of Justin's gait. He always put a little extra weight on his right foot, and it gave me a filthy idea.

"Who do you think that is?" I opened her bodice the rest of the way, then tweaked her nipples into stiff peaks. "I bet he'd sure like to see you so beautifully flushed like this and about to come on my hand."

Her eyes widened and I laid my free hand over her lips as the door cracked open. Instead of revealing her gorgeous body, I blocked the view until I was absolutely sure it was Justin. When he peeked around the corner, I relaxed.

"What do we have here?" he asked, stepping into the tack room. He closed the door and blocked it with a wooden trunk. "Looks like a wife in need of her husbands' attention."

"I believe you're right." Stepping back, I switched places with him.

She opened her mouth and he kissed her, cutting off whatever she was about to say as I glanced around the small storage area. There had to be something... I smirked when my eyes lit on a saddle rack and a pile of blankets. It was just what we needed.

I locked eyes with Justin as I moved it into the center of the room and covered it with a few horse blankets. Still kissing her, he walked Maddy backward until her hip met the saddle rack.

"You two," she said, breathing hard. Her pretty green eyes were clouded with passion. "I declare—"

"Shh." I laid a finger over her pouting lips. "You don't want someone to come in for real, do you?"

"Maybe you'd like that," Justin replied, bending her over the blankets. He pushed her skirts aside and touched her dripping pussy, then held up wet fingers. "You're soaked at just the thought."

He dropped to his knees behind her, then shouldered her knees apart before burying his face in her searing heat.

Stiffening, she cried out, her lips parting. I bent down and kissed her to keep her quiet. She shuddered under Justin's expert touch, her body quaking as he gave her the ultimate delight.

My cock ached and I fisted it through my trousers as she

sobbed out the last of her climax. "I think she needs more," I gritted out.

Justin rose to his feet, his jaw hard as he adjusted himself. "So do we."

"Please..." Maddy lifted her torso off the blankets, giving us a beseeching look. "I need you."

"Then that's what you'll have." I unfastened my trousers, freeing my hard shaft as Justin did the same behind her. Holding her hair, I gently lifted her head to brush her soft lips with the head of my cock.

She opened her mouth and suckled me, pulling me deep as her hands went to my hips. Lord have mercy, it had been too long. Closing my eyes, I threw my head back as she slurped at my hard shaft, her tongue teasing the sensitive crown.

"Look at how beautiful you are," Justin crooned, stroking her back. Her dress slid off her shoulders, revealing pale skin peppered with a few fading bruises. They still made me furious, but I couldn't think about it now. "I wish you could see how lovely you are with Caleb's thick cock in your mouth."

"Do you need Justin in your sweet pussy, Maddy?" Pins fell free as I loosened her hair and wrapped the silky mass around my fist. "Do you need him to fuck you while you're bent over with my cock in your mouth?"

She moaned around me, the vibration making my balls tighten as Justin eased his cock into her tight channel. I wished I could see, but the voluminous pile of pale green silk skirts blocked my view.

I slowed my movement, fucking her mouth with languid strokes. I didn't want to come too soon, but we couldn't stay locked in here all day. She bucked between us, making

Justin hiss out a breath, and her hands tightened on my belt to pull me closer.

"You're going to come for us, Maddy. Cover my cock with your honey while we fill you with our seed." Bending over her, he reached under her skirts, making her cry out and suck me harder. "You're going to spend the entire trip home with a plug in your bottom so we can make you ours the minute we get back."

Jerking, she spasmed and convulsed around us. Her sweet mouth milked the cum from my balls in a furious rush and my knees almost buckled as I exploded into her.

Justin let out a soft growl as his hips thrust against her, pushing her down on my sensitive shaft. His head went back and he stilled, his hand still busy under her skirts. She quivered and whined softly as she released me from the warm cavern of her mouth.

Her hands fell from my belt and she drooped over the saddle rack, sweat glistening on her forehead. She panted for a moment, then caught her breath.

"You two," she murmured. "I declare."

Laughing softly, we put our clothes to rights, then helped her repair her appearance as best we could. Swinging her into my arms, I carried her to the house.

"Miss Maddy!" Sara cried, catching us as we walked in. "What happened? Did that no-account Nathan—"

"No," I said soothingly, pressing Maddy's head against my shoulder. "She just got a little carried away and did too much. I'll lay her down for a short nap, and she'll be right as rain before supper."

"I swear, you and Justin are going to drive me to an asylum," she muttered, not protesting when I took her to her room and tucked her in.

"You weren't complaining earlier," I countered, leaning down to brush my lips across her forehead.

Letting out a soft sigh, she closed her eyes, a tiny, secret smile bowing her lips upward. "Can't wait to get home."

Leaving her to sleep, I went to help Caleb with the packing. I wanted to be on a train before the end of the week.

———

MADDY

A FULL WEEK after my arrival in Kentucky, we were finally on our way home. This train ride was so much different from my last one. For one thing, I was wearing a proper dress and corset, and my hair was pinned under a neat straw hat. I also had quite a bit more luggage, along with furniture, linens, my mother's china packed in straw, and everything else I'd need to set up a comfortable household.

It was the dowry I should have had in the first place, but I had no idea where I was going to put everything. My protests fell on deaf ears. Caleb and Justin simply packed everything Sara told them to. Despite my reservations, it would be nice to have my own familiar belongings.

Although the bruises on my face had faded to a bilious yellow, I still caught my husbands scowling at them when they thought I wasn't looking. It wasn't their fault. Who would have guessed my innocent letter to Mr. Fuller would have caused such trouble?

Aside from the huge pile of things my husbands packed, we had a private compartment on the train. It was a luxury

I'd never expected, but welcomed. Best of all, it gave us plenty of privacy.

They drove me to distraction with illicit touches and caresses. I spent my days stewing in helpless arousal, exacerbated by the wooden toy firmly plugging my bottom hole. Despite my pleas, they refused to make love to me. The one thing they hadn't packed had been my drawers. I had nothing but constant dripping need covering my private parts.

As we passed through St. Louis, my husbands finally broached the subject I hadn't wanted to talk about.

"What do you plan to do with your father's property?" Justin asked while we ate supper in our compartment.

"Sell it, I suppose. I don't want it."

"It's your childhood home," Caleb reminded me.

"I'm no longer a child." To reinforce my words, I stroked my hand across the bulge in his trousers.

"Naughty," he murmured, lifting my hand away. "We're talking about your home."

"No, we're talking about the place I used to live. My home is with you and Justin." I took a bite of roast chicken, hoping they'd drop the subject. I supposed we needed to discuss it though. Otherwise, it would sit in the back of our heads and nothing would be done about it.

I wanted it gone. But not to someone I didn't like. The thought of Nathan buying it, for example, made my heart hurt. But who?

"I know what I'm going to do," I said, laying my silverware beside my plate. It was the perfect solution, and I had no idea why it hadn't occurred to me before.

"What's that, sweetheart?" Justin asked.

"I'm going to sell it to Dahlia and Reggie for a penny an

acre. They'll care for it, and I'll be happy knowing it's in good hands."

"Why that amount?" Caleb took my hand and kissed it. "You could get much more for it."

"I know, but I don't care about the money. Dahlia and Reggie can afford it, and I think it's a proper reward for helping me get to you."

Caleb shared a glance with Justin, and they nodded. "Done," Caleb finally said. "We'll send Mr. Fuller a letter from our next stop."

14

USTIN

I PULLED Maddy into my lap, nibbling on the tender skin below her ear. We approved wholeheartedly of her idea, and it was time to reward our sweet girl. Spreading her thighs apart, I pulled her skirts up.

Her delicious pussy was already wet and slick for us. She moaned and let her head fall back to my shoulder as Caleb knelt between her knees. I unbuttoned her bodice, baring the swells of her breasts pushed up by her corset into a feast for our senses. Still kissing her throat, I tweaked her nipples, making her squeal and grab Caleb's head, firmly buried between her pale thighs.

My cock jerked in my trousers and I bit back a pained hiss. I couldn't wait to get her home. She'd be completely healed from her misadventure by then, and Caleb and I planned to keep her in bed and naked for at least a week.

She'd be well prepared for us as well, what with the toy inside her almost constantly.

"Fuck her with that plug," I said. "I want to see her come with something in her ass." I kissed her again, cupping her jaw to make her turn her head. "You like having something in your bottom, don't you?"

Her eyes fluttering closed, she breathed out a low groan. "God help me, yes."

"Tell us what you want us to do," Caleb said, lifting his head. His face was coated in her honey and he licked his lips.

Thrashing, she bucked in my arms. "Please, I need you."

"You need a cock inside you, fucking you?" Caleb asked, getting to his feet.

"Please, yes!" Her pale skin flushed a beautiful pink, making my mouth water.

"Say it," I murmured. "Tell us you want our cocks inside you, fucking you."

"I need your cocks inside me," she begged.

"What else?"

"F-fucking me. Please!"

"Such a pretty beg," Caleb murmured, unfastening his trousers. I nodded and helped her sit up. Holding her hair, I made her be still as he eased his shaft into her mouth.

"You're our good girl," I crooned slipping my hand between her thighs to play with the plug in her bottom. Easing it in and out, I fucked her with it while she suckled Caleb's hard cock. Gritting his teeth, he slapped a hand on the wall above our heads, straining toward impending release.

"Going to come," he rasped, his body shuddering as he tried to pull away. Instead of letting him go, Maddy grabbed his belt, holding fast as he exploded down her throat.

Giving us a satisfied smirk, Maddy wiped a trickle of Caleb's seed from the corner of her mouth, then climbed from my lap and knelt between my knees. Her small, delicate hands made short work of my belt buckle and the buttons on my trousers. Green eyes hooded with intent, she said, "Your turn."

"Lord have mercy." I kept my eyes focused on her as she made love to me with her mouth. Caleb crouched behind her, his hand busy between her legs as he crooned sweetly profane words of encouragement in her ear.

I wanted to be gentle with her. This wasn't our intent, yet things had gotten out of hand. When I tried to pull away, desperate for release, she sank her short nails into my thigh, then swallowed me down. I shouted my release, uncaring that everyone in the Pullman car probably heard.

She let out a tiny squeak and her eyes fell shut as she shuddered. Her head dropped to my knee as she panted out her delight.

"Maddy mine," I choked out, petting her mussed coiffure.

"Maddy... ours," Caleb countered, helping her settle on the bench between us.

"Maddy yours," she whispered, nestling against us.

———

CALEB

THE TRIP WAS a hedonist's delight, filled with delectable food, decadent touch, and connection between Maddy, Justin, and me on the most basic level. I almost didn't want it to end, but I was too eager to get our wife home and make her our wife in truth.

Her face was bright and cheerful as we crossed into Montana Territory, the bruises nearly faded from her gorgeous face. She was as excited to get home as we were. I smiled. Likely, she looked forward to seeing Prince, but I couldn't fault her for it.

When we arrived in Bridgewater the next day, I blinked at the crowd waiting for the train. Heavens! Why were there so many people?

"Mercy! Is President Cleveland doing a whistle-stop tour?" Maddy turned to us, a luminous smile on her face. "Do you think he's on our train?"

"That would be a fine thing," Justin said, gathering our belongings in preparation. "You might get to shake his hand."

When the train pulled to a stop, we disembarked, Maddy walking contentedly between us. A woman's voice called out, "Maddy May!"

"No, Maddy Mathis." I recognized Robert's voice and turned, grinning as he held Ann back.

"It's still May and she's come back to us. Let go of me, you beast!"

Laughing, he released her, and she rushed straight into Maddy's embrace. Tears poured down Maddy's face as they hugged each other. "It's so good to be home," she choked out.

My chest tightened and I rubbed the sore spot over my ribs. Our wife had been right. Home wasn't a place. It was wherever Maddy and Justin were. Our neighbors surrounded us, filling the air with good cheer and congratulations for bringing her back.

The men of Bridgewater unloaded Maddy's belongings

into wagons, promising to deliver them to our ranch. I sighed with happy resignation, knowing we'd have to add a room or two to the house where we would hopefully be raising a family soon.

Dashiell McPherson clapped me on the shoulder. "Good work bringing that sweet girl home," he murmured, watching the ladies of Bridgewater take Maddy in hand. "Your ranch was well-tended while you were gone, but I'm afraid that stallion of hers is a randy beast. You'll have a right mess of foals come spring." Shaking his head, he chuckled. "Caught two of my mares when Rebecca and I were out there."

The crowd followed us home, bringing food and drink for a celebration. Someone even had a fiddle and we danced with our wife until the stars lit up the wide Montana sky like diamonds in a vast sea of velvet.

Late snow dusted us as if in blessing. Maddy spun, catching snowflakes on her tongue that melted in the warm spring air before they hit the ground. I swallowed, trying to ease the ache in my chest at the thought of how close we'd come to losing her.

A hard hand clasped mine, our fingers lacing together as we watched her joy. "She's home," Justin murmured.

"Safe," I agreed. "And we'll never let her go."

———

MADDY

MADDY MAY. I chuckled at my new name. It struck me funny, but seemed apropos. May was associated with ancient celebration; the time of rebirth and burgeoning life.

Did I not have a new life here under the protective shelter of wild Montana mountains with two men I loved to distraction?

Imagine that. I'd have been happy with a husband I didn't actively hate. Instead, I had two magnificent men I was proud to call mine. And tonight, I'd be theirs, body and soul. I couldn't wait.

Our guests drifted away, wives safely in the arms of their husbands as they left. I let out a happy sigh as the last of them made their way home. Although I was thrilled at the welcome I'd received, I looked forward to being alone with my husbands.

I waved the last of our visitors away, then went inside. Justin stood at the kitchen sink, washing his bare torso. Muscles flexed in his back under smooth ebony skin, begging for my touch.

My core dampened and my limbs went boneless with surging desire as I walked to him, loosening the buttons on my bodice. "Let me," I murmured, taking the cloth from him.

Caleb joined us, bare but for a towel draped across his broad shoulders. Sprawling lazily in a kitchen chair, he fisted his thick cock, rubbing his thumb over the swollen crown as he watched me bathe Justin. My breath hitched in my throat and I nearly dropped the cloth.

"I wish I hadn't been in such a hurry to wash," he murmured, his voice a low baritone that made my insides twitch in response.

His skin glistening with moisture, Justin took the cloth from me. "We should show her the surprise."

"What surprise?"

"Why, I think you're right," Caleb replied, ignoring my question. Grinning a Lucifer smile, he tugged my dress away, baring me to my husbands' avid perusal. Without giving me a chance to protest, they bundled me in a blanket. The next thing I knew, I was astride Prince, Justin behind me. His cock was so hot against my bottom, and between the movement of my horse between my legs and his presence behind me, I couldn't say a word in my defense.

Caleb vaulted to his mare's back and led the way across the darkened pastures to a hidden recess under the escarpment I hadn't had time to explore.

Steam rose from a small pool, smelling faintly of minerals and sulphur. I gasped in pleasure as Justin helped me down, then let the blanket fall away and dipped my toe into the hot water.

"You never told me of this," I murmured. I couldn't decide whether to castigate them for not showing me this magical place, or kiss them soundly for the surprise. I supposed it was better they hadn't told me. I'd have likely spent every waking hour soaking in the hot water.

"It was supposed to be a gift on the night we took you fully," Caleb said, helping me into the pool.

I groaned as I sank into the hot water. "I love Montana," I breathed.

"And we love you, Maddy May," Justin whispered settling into the water next to me, turning my face so he could kiss me.

My heart nearly burst and tears pricked my eyes. I wasn't sure I'd ever cried so much in my life, but these were tears of joy. Such happiness must be a sin, but I'd grab it with both hands and thank the Lord for every moment.

"Are you ready for us?" Caleb asked, kneeling at my feet.

"More than ready." I laid hands on their dear faces, pulling them close. "Make me yours."

They took me from the pool and laid me on the blanket

under a brilliant full moon. I felt wanton and lush, like I was a pagan priestess anticipating tribute. Caleb stretched out on his back next to me, then helped me straddle his hips.

His cock nudged at my entrance, making me shiver with need. I wanted them so badly, I was sure I'd die from it.

"Take him inside you," Justin urged. His huge hand wrapped around my neck, making me feel both comforted and bound to his will.

I lowered myself, relishing the stretch of his thickness. Justin pushed me down gently until my chest pressed against Caleb's. I loved the heat of him so close to my body.

Cool liquid trickled down, coating me in slickness as Justin knelt behind me and eased his fingers into my bottom. Mercy, it felt...incomparable. I lacked the words to describe the sensation of both of them taking me in the most intimate way possible in this magical place existing a step out of reality.

"Please," I whispered. "Make me yours."

The stretch of Justin's hard shaft entering me hurt at first, but it was a delicious hurt, both stretching and strangely filling. Fulfilling and debauched, decadent and absolutely, perfectly right.

———

JUSTIN

Leaning down, I kissed Maddy's soft shoulder, trailing my tongue across her silken skin to the sweet spot behind her ear. If someone had told me even half a year ago I would find the most perfect woman in the world, I'd have called them a damned liar.

Yet here she was in our embrace.

Accepting, welcoming, kind, and more beautiful than the stars. Our Maddy May.

She clenched tight, her body welcoming me into hers until I thought I might lose my breath for the want of her. I eased myself into her bottom, gritting my teeth against the urge to thrust. I wouldn't hurt her for the world.

Letting out a soft groan, she pushed back against me. Sinking my fingers into the soft flesh of her hips, I fucked her with long, leisurely strokes, feeling Caleb's member slide against mine, separated only by a thin membrane as she rocked between us.

Her pale skin gleamed, pristine and gilded with the light from the full moon as she writhed, her lips parted with desire. She was perfect. And she was ours.

She arched her back, her hands on Caleb's chest as she cried out her pleasure. Beads of sweat sparkled like gems on her skin and she flushed pink as she spasmed.

Tendons straining in his neck, Caleb reached up to tweak her nipples, making her shudder. Her nails dug crescent indentations into his chest as she screamed, sending the sound of her joy to the heavens.

Tightening around me, her channel drew me in, dragging the seed from my balls in a tremendous rush. I couldn't stop it, nor did I want to. The clench of the heart of her pulling me into her body was too much to bear. She was all silken softness and strength, our wanted bride.

I collapsed, rolling away so I didn't crush her. My lungs worked like a bellows, and I wheezed as I tried to catch my breath. She stretched out a hand, and I leaned into her touch as she stroked my face.

"I love you," she whispered solemnly, curling up

between us with her leg thrown over Caleb's hip. "Both of you."

"We love you too," Caleb replied, reaching for the end of the blanket to cover her. "You're our dream come true."

We bathed our sweet Maddy May in the hot spring, trusting the mineral rich water to soothe her. Languid and drowsy, she dozed as we tended to her, then fell asleep in my arms before we reached home. I handed her down to Caleb, and he carried her inside while I turned the horses loose.

The spring air chased a chill over my bare skin, but I paid it no mind and knelt in the grass. Movement behind me announced the presence of my best friend, and he joined me on the ground.

I took his hand, twining my fingers with his. "I thought I'd send up a prayer of thanks."

He nodded, bowing his head. "Thank you, Lord, for giving us Maddy."

"And for bringing her back to us safely," I added.

A shooting star crossed the sky, making me wish she could see it.

"We're supposed to wish on a falling star," Caleb said, his voice reverent.

"No need." I stood, pulling him up with me. "We have everything we could have ever wanted."

BRIDGEWATER BRIDES

Want more Bridgewater Brides?
See the full list of books in the world:
http://bridgewaterbrides.com/books/

Be sure to sign up for the world newsletter to stay up to date
on new releases:
http://bridgewaterbrides.com/mailing-list/

ABOUT RAISA GREYWOOD

Author of filthy smut, empty nester, and cat snuggler.
She's worked as a teacher, an actuary (her husband called
her a bookie—which isn't too far from the truth), mother,
scout leader, and is now enjoying semi-retirement writing
the books she always wanted to read.

———

Join the Raunchy Renegades at https://www.facebook.com/
groups/272762356598383/.

You can also sign up for her newsletter at https://www.
subscribepage.com/bridgewater.

As a bonus, everyone who signs up will receive a FREE
exclusive Bridgewater short story based on the events in
Their Wanted Bride.

Facebook: https://www.
facebook.com/AuthorRaisaGreywood/

Twitter: https://twitter.com/Raisa_Greywood
Instagram: https://www.instagram.com/raisagreywood/
Website: https://raisagreywood.com/

ALSO BY RAISA GREYWOOD

Dad Bod Doms

Henry

Happily Never After (written with Sinistre Ange)

Demon Lust

Blood Lust

Holiday Daddy Doms

Jennifer's Christmas Daddy

A Valentine for Chelsea

Shifter's Mates

The Tiger Queen

The Tiger King

The Leopard Mage

The Leopard Prince

The Jaguar Rogue

The Jaguar Knight

Standalone Titles & Anthologies

Longing and Lust & Other Short Stories

Bastard's New Baby

Ladder 54: Five Firefighter Romances

Masters of the Castle: Witness Protection Program

Dangerous Curves Ahead: An Anthology

Wicked Magic

Wicked Deception

Wicked Truth

Wicked Fire